WESTSIDE TITANOMACHY

MIDLIFE OLYMPIANS: THE ORACLE CHRONICLES #4

T.J. DESCHAMPS

EDITED BY
EMILY PAPER

WITCH WORKS PUBLISHING, LLC

DEDICATION

For my adult (and almost an adult!) children...and anyone who reads
this book:
There is no such thing as fate. We all have a chance to write our own
stories. However, never forget we don't write a single word alone. We
need friends, family (especially chosen), and community in every
chapter.

Love, Ma (T.J.)

PROLOGUE

Dione struggled against the chains as the two Titans dragged her from the Null to the all too familiar dais. Instead, Zeus's smug face on the throne, she met the gaze of her erstwhile co-conspirator. His mother Leto and Hera sat on his left and on his right, Cronus and...her heart shattered. There, on the former thrones of the Twelve sat four of the children she'd once abandoned.

Crumbling to her knees, the Titan hung from her shackles held by her captors as she wept with joy for her beloved children's freedom, but also in agony, for the ones who were seated on the thrones and among the crowd gathered behind. They all despised her.

"Oh, stop your whining," Apollo drawled in a bored voice, strumming his lyre. "They want you gone, but I convinced them to not to destroy someone so useful."

The taunting pulled Dione to her feet and straightened her spine. Mustering composure, she stared into the god's pretty, treacherous face. "Useful to whom?"

Like a teenager, he rolled his eyes. "Really, Dione. You've survived this long in your enemy's court." He gestured to Hera, who stiffened at the remark. "Yet, you pretend that you don't know why you're more useful alive than dead to all present?"

She lifted her chin. "I will not serve you. You are no longer the god of music and poetry. You are the god of deception and lies."

Apollo continued to strum his wretched lyre, eyeing her as if she were a petulant child, not someone he'd betrayed again and again. But wasn't she also just as deceptive? She'd had her machinations, too.

A sharp steel band clamped around her heart. Considering her descendant's lives less worthy than her first children, she'd sacrificed so many of her line in hope of freeing the ones she'd betrayed so long ago from Tartarus. She and Apollo had tricked many of her kin together until she realized he didn't want to usurp Zeus and rule Olympus. She glared at him. He'd wanted to ascend and leave everything in shambles—an Olympus and Earth worse than Tartarus. She'd thought Hera and the others wanted Zeus out for all the wrongs he'd done to them, but all of them had the same agenda to be omnipotent and omniscient beings. Flawed as she may be, Dione didn't want to lose all of who she was in exchange for ultimate power.

"I offer you more than service. I offer you true immortality."

She furrowed her brow but let him continue to speak.

"You, Lydia, and Luke will replace the Moirai."

Dione forgot her personal gripe with the god. "You cannot replace the Fates. They are—"

"Personifications of a concept," Cronus finished. His voice boomed in her ears even though he spoke in a mild tone. *How had he retained so much power?* "They are but Oracles given the responsibility. Like any god or goddess of whatever concept, they can be replaced."

This intrigued Dione. Currently, she had no place anywhere except to serve a god she despised. As a Fate, she would hold the power. Everyone would listen to her again, even her enemies.

However, she decided to pretend she was against the idea. If

Apollo knew this intrigued her, he would know he had the upper hand. "They know you've planned this. They can see what you'll try. You won't be able to do it."

"The trouble with locking yourself in a realm made of the tapestry of Fate is that you cannot leave it. They will see what we shall do, but they can do nothing to stop it," Apollo replied.

"What's in it for you?" Dione asked, her gaze passing over the new and old rulers of Olympus.

Apollo leaned forward, a gleam of something she couldn't read in his eyes. "No more prophecies. No more touching the eyes of your mortal descendants to allow them to see the future. If they want to know the future, they'll have to pray to me."

"Why would they do that?"

"Because I am going to start a war that will have every single being wanting to know what will happen, who to side with, and they will learn from the current Oracle the only way to stop it is to bow down and pray to me."

Dione ignored the young god's smug expression. Instead, she focused her gaze on Cronus. He met her stare with a slight smirk.

A shiver ran through her.

Cronus's smile was never good. She didn't need to read the Titan's thread to know that whatever Apollo had planned, Uranus was only biding his time to decide what *he* wanted to do. The beautiful, but dumb god should have kept to the arts.

ONE

My eyes focused on the sand pierced by the spear Athena had thrown, I hefted the javelin over my shoulder. In my harpy form I could meet the goddess's throw, but I was not. Training in both forms meant I would be prepared to fight without the pause to shift. Getting good at long range weapons would give me that crucial time to shift into my other form for close range battle.

Others trained at different things all around me. Zeus and Hermes spun circles around each other. Their swords clattering before my vision could register the movement.

Dressed in full armor, Athena gestured with her Aegis—a shield with a gorgon's bronzed head. Medusa, who betrayed her. I didn't know the full story. Arachne said the myth everyone knew about the gorgon was too petty for Athena and made up by men who didn't understand the motives of women let alone goddesses.

Still, I hated looking at the gruesome thing. At least it didn't turn anyone to stone.

Athena tapped my shoulder. "Remember your form."

"Right." I adjusted myself in the proper stance. Supernatural or not, my muscles had to learn this technique. Years of sitting my butt in a fortuneteller's chair had made me soft. Three years of training for a war that might or might not come had changed that. I still had curves, but my arms and legs developed muscle. My core strength improved, and my coordination got better and better.

Executing the practiced movement, I heaved the javelin. The rod launched from my fingers into the air, arched and fell short of Athena's mark by a long shot. My heart sank.

Athena shouted, "Excellent. Again!"

It didn't feel excellent. No matter how far I'd come, I still had so far to go to defend against an attack. However, I didn't have time to mope about it. I picked up another javelin and did as she commanded. Again and again until I couldn't lift my arm. Still, I came nowhere near the casual toss of an Olympian.

The goddess clapped me on the shoulder. "You've made good progress at distance. Soon we will move on to throwing at a target, then a moving target."

She saw my sour look and amended, "You needn't be the best at using a spear as a weapon. Just good enough to shift to harpy form in a surprise attack."

"What if I don't have a javelin on me?" I put all my worries into the tone of that question.

Athena considered me for a moment before answering, "You're learning to buy yourself time to get away. Anything will do."

"I doubt I'll do much damage with anything."

Then the goddess clapped my other shoulder so all I could see was her face. "You are not training to defend this world like the other harpies. This is for your own personal protection. When the Titanomachy comes, we will be too busy to defend you."

Telling me I only had to be good enough to not be a liability stung more than if Athena had told me that I was crap at this and would never improve. Tears stung my eyes.

Athena's face and tone softened. "Sometimes surviving is all we can do. Stop trying to be the hero that defeats Apollo and start planning to do what it takes to live. That's the difference between us and them. We don't want glory. We want to live to see another day and save as many lives as we can in the process."

I knew this wasn't lip service. When her uncle Poseidon challenged her for rule of Athens, Athena won, but shared the rule over it anyway. We would fight against her kin once again...my kin. Dione was missing. Her intentions were still unclear. I wanted the chance to talk to her, to understand why she put my mother and others to the test. Why she'd let Luke almost die opening the gates. Part of me wanted my only living blood relative other than my son to not be a bad guy.

I'd had enough of them for a several lifetimes.

THE HOT WATER pelted my skin. I opened my mouth, rinsing out some of the grit from the training in sand. A familiar knock made my stomach flutter.

Hermes peeked inside. "Lydia, may I come in?"

We'd been together three years, and he still asked. Still respected my time and my privacy.

"Sure, carota."

A low chuckle sent warmth through my middle. The god stepped in the bathroom and shut the door behind him. Instead of opening the shower curtain, he leaned against the counter. "My sister is concerned that when the time comes, you will make some sort of self-sacrifice to win against Apollo."

I closed my eyes and let the water run over my head, soaking my curls and drowning out all noise. When I finally came up for air, the door clicked shut. I was alone. As much as I wanted Hermes's company, I needed space to think. War loomed over our heads like the sword of Damocles every minute of every day. The thing was, I'd been considering giving myself over to Apollo so I could turn around and murder him. It was a piss poor plan. He hadn't acted alone.

There were Olympians and Titans on his side. This limbo couldn't last forever, but it could last a long time. I only hoped we were prepared when he finally made his move.

My bed was warm and soft as I tucked myself in next to Hermes. Hands cradling the back of his head, the god stared up at the ceiling. I rested a hand on his chest over his heart. I was so exhausted; I could just close my eyes. However, I needed to talk to Hermes and assure him I wasn't going to do anything stupid. Perhaps we could come up with a plan to force Apollo into action together.

"Athena was right. I did plan on doing something, but it would be futile. I was thinking—"

The room grew hazy as if a fog had rolled in. Or was it my head? A vision pushed its way in without my bidding it so. I'd gained control of my Oracular gift, and now fought the oncoming vision. I controlled when and how I saw the future, picking the threads when I chose. Still, the prophecy lurked at the edges of my conscious mind threatening to seek any hole in my mental defenses. No. I was done being pushed around. This was *my* life.

"Lydia?" Hermes voice filled so much tenderness and concern into that one word.

"A Vision," I managed to say between panting breaths. Fighting the Fates when they wanted you to see something was no easy task.

"Is it coming from touching me?"

I shook my head and replied through gritted teeth, "No." At least, I didn't think it was. It felt more like the dreams that came to me when I wasn't in control of my gift.

The beautiful god adjusted himself in the bed to face me. His bold features a mask of worry as he asked, "Are the Moirai trying to tell you something?"

"Maybe?" It was hard to speak, fight the vision and ward off sleep. The day had been a lot. However, if I went to sleep, I had no defenses against whatever direction the Fates wanted to steer ship Lydia. I'd done a lot of homework at Nicky's gymnasium and through my mother's library. I was inextricably tied to Clotho, Lachesis, and

Atropos, but I didn't have to take their visions the same way I could put a call to voicemail.

"This is not a game of wills, Lydia. They cannot use you and have no need to. Any vision the Moirai send is important. You can choose how to act upon what they send, or not take their message at all, but it will only work to your detriment." His voice was calm and reasonable, which made me feel extremely unreasonable for fighting it.

What was I afraid of?

War, chaos, losing everything so that Apollo could become so powerful that he was omnipotent and omnipresent, just to name a few. However, would not listening to the Fates prevent any of this? No, it would not.

I blew out my breath in the longest, most exasperated sigh I'd ever heaved. Woe was Lydia.

"Carlo ran my life for so long. Then, it felt like I was pushed and pulled between the gods and Titans. I want to have control over my life, not some predestined path set by somebody pulling the strings." It sounded silly. Hermes knew that I knew that even when you saw the future, a single action could splinter the threads into many possibilities.

"No one wants to feel like that. No one with any sort of self-worth. You value your time and yourself much more than when we first met and you threw yourself from a building."

I scowled and poked him in the chest. "I was jumping to the next building to get away."

"The Lydia I know now wouldn't have signed her name in blood to anyone or anything. You're no longer scared and running from your problems. You'd face the mundane authorities and tell them exactly what happened, understanding that you did nothing wrong. Seeing a possible future won't change that."

He was right and he was wrong. Not so deep down I already knew the vision would be something awful.

My eyes stung and I swallowed hard. "I'm afraid of what they'll show me."

"Zeus allowed Apollo the throne. We avoided the calamity you predicted."

"We avoided *that* catastrophe," I corrected, releasing a shaky breath.

Hermes brushed my cheek with the back of his hand, wiping away the dampness I hadn't realized was there.

How long had I been crying?

He clasped my face in his big hands. "Whatever you see in the vision. Whatever terrible future is possible, we'll face it, together."

A small smile touched my lips, as I nodded. Hermes had my back. So did all my friends. They had all proven it. That's what I feared, though. I feared seeing myself lose all that I'd gained.

TWO

I stood in a verdant forest unlike any I'd ever seen before. Trees, taller than skyscrapers, towered above me. Their leaves as big as my house, blotting out the sky. Yet, somehow there was a gentle glow illuminating the bushes, ferns, vines, and flowering plants that surrounded me. Although lush and verdant flora bloomed all around, the forest showed none of the telltale signs of fauna. No rustling. No birds chirping. Nothing chittering or chattering. Silence.

"Hello?"

Before me, a thread of golden light appeared, revealing a path. Not knowing what else to do, I followed the thread. The path led to a circular, open-air structure with marble Doric columns supporting a marble domed roof. Inside the structure, three women sat on stools. One spun a golden thread like the one I followed. Another measured it and then fed it into the forest. The ground absorbed the thread and a tiny green shoot sprung from the ground. The third woman reached down, into an unseen place. A root lifted and met her hand. The root unraveled forming into a golden thread. Then, the woman retrieved thread and cut it with a pair of weaver's shears. One of the gargantuan leaves above withered and turned to ash, crumbling to the forest floor.

Concept goddesses in the flesh, Clotho, Lachesis, and Atropos, known as the Fates or the Moirai, went about their work in flowing chitons. Loose, gauzy material covered their hair. I couldn't determine whether they appeared old or young. They had an ageless quality that seemed to shift every time I laid eyes upon each.

My pulse raced and I felt cold all over. I'd met plenty of gods, but never ones as powerful as these three. Why and how they allowed me here, a place no god or Titan dared tread, I didn't know. I didn't move. I didn't dare. This place was not for me, not for anyone, but them, the Fates.

Besides, I feared stomping on an errant flower would cause someone their untimely demise. Part of me chastised my past self for so carelessly wandering in the tapestry of people's lives. It was silly, because I didn't know, but I still felt awful about it.

Clotho looked up from her spinning. Eyes with bottomless depths snared me in their gaze. She paused what she was doing to beckon me. "Lydia, come."

I couldn't move. My feet just wouldn't obey. Too much relied on me not doing any harm.

Without so much as a glance in my direction, the one I assumed was Lachesis scolded, "Don't dawdle, child of the ichor."

Atropos looked at me. Her notice felt like taking a nosedive into a pool of ice water—shocking, painful, and suffocating. I would do anything to be relieved of it. Since doing what the others had bid seemed the only option to escape her stare, I would have to get over my fear of doing harm.

Dread pooling in my stomach, I advanced to the pillared structure. There, I stood between the doric columns, resting a hand on one and surprised by the cool, solid surface. I inhaled and exhaled, breathing in the scent of a forest, marble, and the three incarnations of the Fates. Nothing about this screamed vision. I'd found myself in a world where concept became material.

Clotho held me in her gaze. Of the three, she was the least difficult to look at. However, perceiving her wasn't pleasant. Invisible needles pricked my skin. The inevitably of whatever she would say materialized as a heavy yoke upon my shoulders. The pressing weight of it almost impossible to bear.

The gauzy wrap covering her hair shifted, shadowing her face. "Why are you so fearful? You've been here many times and plucked tales from the weave of the skein. All Oracles have."

The other two sisters nodded and murmured words of agreement.

Is this where my mind went when I read the weave? Was a part of me here as I was now, and I wasn't aware of it?

"Stop musing and answer," Clotho chided.

"I feared doing unintentional damage." It was a partial truth. It wouldn't make sense to say I feared them. They did no one harm. Clotho simply snipped one's existence from the fabric of the forest. She didn't actually end the life.

While I mused, the three exchanged glances, communicating silently. They carried on this exchange for hours, or perhaps seconds? Time seemed ever present and yet to not pass at all.

Finally, Lachesis stepped off the dais and reached her hand out. A thread shot from the ground and into her grip. She then extended the glowing thread to me. "Take."

With no small amount of trepidation, I did as she bid.

When I took this thread into my hand, it wasn't like following the last. I sensed the life within it and how the thread's fibers stopped being individual and became entangled with the manifestation of a forest. Everything glowed, illustrating what I came to understand holding it.

"Yes. Yes. We are all connected," Lachesis explained, sounding impatient. "That's not what we wanted you to know."

"What then?" I asked.

All three Moirai surrounded me. There was no movement. They were simply all there.

Okay. That was freaky.

Clotho covered her face with her hands. "See without your eyes. Listen with your heart. The ichor in your veins will guide you."

I took a deep breath and closed my eyes. A myriad of snippets from people's lives rushed in too fast for me to grasp any meaning out of what was presented. The onslaught of imagery made my head spin. Bile rose in my throat.

"Control what the weave shows you, or it will control you," Atropos warned, her voice distant.

I willed the magic inside me to *see* the weave. The incoming wave of images slowed and stopped as I picked a singular string. There, I saw through someone else's eyes a typical kitchen in a cramped apartment. Their thoughts became mine.

My hand twisted the rag, wiping out my favorite coffee mug. Movement caught my eye, I looked up. Like two planets caught in the other's orbit, two giant balls of fired revolved around each other. At the same time, the burning masses hurtled toward the building across the street. My gaze swept to the phone on the counter. I needed to warn Caleb.

The crash thundered in my ears. The building around me trembled. Then, everything went black.

"Keep going," Atropos urged.

I'm in a park surrounded a massive city. Skyscrapers tower around. Traffic, shouts, and chatter are the soundtrack of my day out with my husband and our daughter. The scents of spices from the street vendor's carts mingles with the more delicate scent of flowers and cut grass. I'm hungry. We'll eat soon. I want...

Old folks practice Qi Gong. Their slow and fluid movements are soothing to watch and reassuring. I smile to myself. That will be me and my love one day, when our daughter is grown and has children of her own. We will retire.

My daughter toddles toward the elders. I let her. We go to this park often and they don't mind her presence. Suddenly she stops and her little cherry mouth opens, forming the cutest circle. She raises her chubby baby fist and points to the sky.

Following her finger, my stomach lurches.

Everyone seems to look up at the same time. Someone shouts to run. I can't, I'm transfixed by what I see.

Balls of fire zip through the air. The flames douse, morphing into the shapes of people with strange, hulking bodies and glowing eyes. They pull weapons. Lightning crackles between the newcomers.

The elderly scatter as fast as their wizened bodies will take them. Some fall.

Winds whip my hair about, nearly knocking me over. The ground trembles under my feet, unsteadying me further. I'm screaming, running, walking, stumbling for my daughter. There is nothing I can do to protect her from this fight but grab her up in my arms and shield her with my own body.

My husband wraps his arms around us both. No words pass between us before blinding light precedes all-consuming flames.

More scenes like this unfolded. All around the world, mundanes became casualties of a conflict they had no part in. Supernaturals, who made any attempt to fight back, ended up embroiled in the war, making the collateral damage greater in the process.

Unable to take any more of the senseless slaughter, I opened my eyes and wiped away the tears that had soaked my cheeks while I watched the people of my world annihilated.

"How can I stop this?"

The Moirai exchanged glances. Atropos spoke, "You cannot. These deaths are inevitable. Unless..." She looked at the sister closest to her and nodded.

Sadness filled Lachesis's features. "Unless..."

Clotho sighed. "Unless you find a way to divert Apollo's attention and prevent the war."

"How and for how long?" At this point, I'd thought of a million ways of how I could kill him, but not how to provide a peaceful means of starting the war in the first place. What could possibly divert a god from executing something he'd planned so long?

"You must be clever, Lydia," Clotho admonished.

"He is a young god. Easily amused. Find an entertainment to divert him." Lachesis extended her hand, palm up.

"You sound like I should ask him to play Parcheesi." I handed her the thread.

Lachesis bent over and allowed the thread to be reabsorbed in ground. Straightening, she said, "If you feel that Parcheesi is challenging enough to divert him. Then do so."

"Yes. Play a game. Win the game," Atropos agreed. Her eternal eyes limned with...was that worry? "Or, we all lose."

CHAPTER

THREE

The Supernatural Council of the Americas, accompanied by their two enforcers, once again sat in my dining room, along with my household of gods and supernaturals. We also had the company of I.S.E.A agents Tan and Roanhorse. They listened in quiet horror as I recalled the possible futures shown to me by the Moirai.

"Every thread showed catastrophic consequences of an earth-bound battle. The Fates instructed me to divert Apollo and said I had to act before he did."

Everyone present stared. Not one face seemed untroubled by what I'd shared. Quite the opposite. Worry etched their features. The shock of the potential annihilation of mundanes and supes alike stunned everyone into silence.

"Did the visions give any clue as to when these attacks would take place?" Agent Tan asked, breaking the second round of silence.

My answer was immediate, because I'd replayed the encounter in my mind repeatedly looking for any clue that would tell me exactly that. "I didn't see any calendars, phones, or clocks."

"Any seasonal decorations?" Miriam asked, tilting her white antlered head to one side.

Encouraged by the fae witch's line of questioning, our fearless leader of the supernatural council, Gabriel, asked, "What was the weather like?"

"Both excellent questions," Zeus encouraged with an approving nod.

Gee, thanks for the support, dad.

I bit my lip considering. "Not all of the visions were the same season. It was winter some places. Summer in others."

A bit of the tension coiling in the room eased. I realized why. It was currently spring where we were in the northern hemisphere. We had time. At least a few months, if not longer. The Fates hadn't given me a when but at least we had some clue.

Finally, Athena, who had kept her peace so far, spoke, "The Moirai specifically asked *you* to *divert* Apollo from starting this war?"

I met her scrutinizing gaze without flinching. Yeah. I could lie. I had made up things for a living, but this time I was telling the truth —even though it was what I confessed to wanting all along. "Yes."

The goddess frowned. "I see."

She exchanged concerned glances with her brother. A muscle in Hermes's cheek feathered, but he kept his peace. Both were concerned I'd do something that would lead to my demise. Hermes had lost many Oracles, their deaths weighed on him, but this time he had a personal attachment. We'd only begun something good, and it might all be lost.

I spread my hands, wanting to assure him and everyone else I wouldn't do anything rash. "The Fates didn't ask me to sacrifice myself or to kill Apollo, only to distract him. We have a lot of brain power here. I thought maybe I could get some advice on how to distract him from the people who know him best."

Athena swung her gaze to the I.S.E.A agents and back to me, subtly lifting her eyebrows.

In answer to her unspoken question of *why invite the mundane authorities,* I said, "As a member of the Supernatural Council, it is my duty to make the mundane authorities aware of potential threats. I'd say this is a pretty big one."

One would think my reasoning would be obvious. However, Athena had no love for the agency after they'd imprisoned me and Luke for Leto and Apollo's crimes. I.S.E.A had their reasons, mainly to get Apollo to act, but he hadn't. He was playing some sort of long game, but it involved the near future.

"Did they give you any insight or a vision that would tell you *how* to distract Apollo?" Phyr asked.

I played back in my mind the conversation I'd had with the Moirai. I didn't want to admit I'd flippantly asked if I should challenge him to a game of Parcheesi. So, I paraphrased. "The Moirai said to play to win."

"Perhaps they meant a literal game," Hermes suggested. "We Olympians love games."

The other gods and supernaturals agreed.

Athena looked at her father. "What if you were to challenge him to a public spectacle for the right to rule Olympus? A series of competitive feats that all mundanes and supernaturals could see."

Zeus stroked his beard. "That sounds like an excellent plan. Avoiding a costly war and a bloodless defeat."

I bit my lip. Control over this plan was getting away from me. I wanted input for how I'd go about this diversion, not for the gods to take over. "That would be perfect except for one thing. Whatever the plan is, it has to involve me."

"Instead of one of you challenging Apollo," Roanhorse gestured at Zeus and then waved his arm indicating everyone at the table except himself and Tan. "Why don't you hold a supernatural Olympics?"

A few of the Olympians raised their eyebrows. Others exchanged questioning glances.

Agent Tan explained further, "We mundanes set aside our wars to compete in athletic games we call the Olympics. The competitions are viewed around the world as they occur, and the athletes are revered by all."

Plenty of adoration points for Apollo and the Titans that would make it appealing. This might be the diversion we need.

"What might we expect as competitions?"

Princess pulled out her phone and brought up a video, holding it up.

"Wait. I have a projector." Tan provided a device that projected the video in a 3D holographic video we could all view.

The video showed short clips of the modern Olympic Games over the last century. When the video ran its course, Athena asked, "You said that humans paused wars to play these games. Why? What was the prize?" Tan amended, "Well, only the wars that hindered the games, but every nation competes."

Arachne, who usually stayed quiet for any sort of meeting, chimed in, "The prizes aren't what matters. It's the glory. It's a point of pride for each country when their teams and individual athletes prove they are superior in both physical prowess and strategic ability."

"So, we invite more than one group of supernatural to compete as a team." This would be a thousand times better than fighting over turf.

"We'll need a prize," Zeus offered. "Something Apollo covets."

All eyes turned to me. "If a challenge against you alone would tempt him, wouldn't the chance to beat all other gods and supernaturals be prize enough?"

Murmurs of agreement followed. Zeus nodded. "Yes. I believe it would."

"Where will these games be held?" Athena asked.

Good question. I wanted wherever these games to be as far from mundanes as possible.

"Would my gymnasium work?" Nicky offered.

"No." Gabriel said in a tone that made it a full sentence that brooked no argument. Adjusting his tone, he then made a suggestion. "What about the Vault?"

No two words could make my blood run cold like the name of the place where we'd spent weeks. It wasn't that the prison where the angels, and later I.S.E.A, kept supernaturals was terrible in a torturous sense, but the monotony and boredom was enough to drive a person mad. To voluntarily put myself there again for longer than a rescue attempt hit me harder than I thought it would.

All eyes were on me though. This was my thing. I wanted to lead it and I must. Swallowing my fear, I asked, "Okay. Why the Vault?"

"The Vault is a prison, but it doesn't have to be. I've done some digging. The interior is through spellwork. We could invite each group to have a representative have a hand in planning and building the staging of the games. Everything would be contained. The Vault can handle a lot of magic casted in one place."

"Can we somehow broadcast what happens there to Earth?" I asked the two I.S.E.A agents.

They exchanged glances. Roanhorse's usual stony expression betrayed...nervousness? The flicker of worry in his eyes happened so fast, I wasn't sure if I'd seen it or imagined it. Tan cleared her throat.

"We had a way of monitoring cells visually, yes." Roanhorse spread his hands. "It will have to be adapted if you change the interior, but I believe the fundamental workings could stay the same." His gaze shifted to Luke.

My son, an I.S.E.A operations agent in training, straightened in his chair. He'd sat among the gods and supernaturals, but he was their person now. "Yeah. We'll have to replace the cameras and some of the magical components to it, but I believe it could be done. I'm more than happy to spearhead monitoring."

I took a long slow breath. My son found a way to be part of this without insisting on being in the competition itself. A lot had changed since he was thrown into the supernatural world. As an I.S.E.A. agent, he saw a lot more of the other supernaturals than I did as someone representing the Greco-Roman pantheon.

Hephaestus raised an arm bulging with muscles—a forger's build. "I could help with the technology and the sporting goods, as well as planning the layout of the games."

The room buzzed with excited energy. Conversations engaged. I needed to bring it back to focus. "Then it is agreed. We will issue challenges to Apollo and the leaders of the supernatural groups?"

Miriam was the only one who didn't agree. Instead, she raised a question. "Are we issuing invitations to Heaven and Hell for this?"

I gave her a rueful smile. "We need both worlds to compete. It's important Apollo feels that he'll miss something if he doesn't show."

Gabriel stiffened at first, but he seemed to accept what I said, slowly nodding his agreement. His eyes went to his partner.

Miriam chewed her lip. No small feat for someone with fangs to not rip the flesh to shreds as she mulled over whatever she was deciding. If Miriam wasn't in, the fae and the witches weren't in.

Thinking it might be easier to discuss what her qualms might be that would have her weighing what should be a no brainer, I gestured to the door. "Can I talk to you alone for a second?"

We left the others in the dining room to discuss the plans. Gabriel squeezed her hand as we passed.

I took her all the way back to my office. It seemed far enough for prying ears, but Miriam whispered something. The door glowed white for a moment and magic pricked my skin.

"I fear what Lucifer will try to gain from an event of this magnitude," she admitted without prompting. She wrung pale, shimmering hands. "I also fear the angels will use the Vault to do something to Gabriel. So much could go wrong." She blew out her breath. "Am I stupid for worrying about my personal problems when so much is at stake?"

I snorted. "When your personal problems involve a powerful archangel and the king of Hell, I think you're allowed to have a few misgivings."

Her coke bottle green eyes met my gaze. "Most of all, I fear my father exacting his revenge. Oberon is more powerful than all of them, but if his light is snuffed out and his higher self goes to the Summerlands, I will be the ruler of a place I'd rather not be. It will spark a war with my siblings akin to what Apollo has planned for this world. The casualties will be great."

I looked at this fae witch and saw beyond the pink hair and antlers, past the ethereal green eyes and the old, old magic that resided within her. Miriam was a person, who for her entire life, has had the weight of everyone's ambitions on her. Still, she worried about how all of this will affect everyone else. "Would you like me to read your thread?" I asked for the very first time. Everyone had always asked me. I'd never offered a reading unsolicited, but I felt Miriam needed some reassurance...or fair warning.

She looked at me for a moment, considering my offer. The green of her eyes grew luminous. That old magic stirred. She closed her eyes, squeezing them shut as if squeezing out an image she didn't want to see or preventing *something* from seeing *me*.

When she finally opened them again, she said a phrase that sounded like it had been learned by rote. "Divination entrenches a path that might otherwise be left untaken."

Got it. She feared knowing her fate would make her act in ways that would make it inevitable. "Thought I'd ask. Eases the mind of some who don't know which path to take."

With a soft smile, she was the suburban mom again, albeit with fae looks. "I appreciate the offer, but no, thank you. I think I need to clear my own path without the aid of future knowledge."

CHAPTER

FOUR

In Delphi, Greece, the ruins of the amphitheater, once known as the Temple of the Pythian Apollo, surrounded me. The limestone seating once held thousands of people for musical and singing competitions. Athena said that the place was Apollo's favorite on earth. Fitting place to record step one in Project Distraction.

The day was bright and sunny. The magic Apollo imbued upon the place still here, faint but beating like an external pulse against my skin.

This wasn't just a place important to the god.

Delphi had been the seat of Pythia and all her descendants, my ancestors. Tears stung the back of my eyes. All of their hopes, dreams, simple wants and grand desires swirled in a corner of my head. I could see what the place once was and what it is now at once. The stark difference almost too much to bear.

Every person who came before me led up to this moment, to me, challenging the god they'd once served. Would my ancestors curse or cheer me for it? Best not to consider the feelings of the dead when the living were at stake. However, a tiny piece of me, the piece who

24

grew up without a mother wanted their approval, their good will, and support.

Athena clasped the owl on her necklace and stretched her arm out, the pendant transformed into a golden owl automaton. The bird perched her on her arm, blinking and ruffling its feathers. Her dark eyes settled on me and she nodded, signifying the owl would record my message.

An olive branch in one hand and a laurel in my other, I took a breath and sealed this moment in my head forever. Either I would look back on it, or Luke would see it as if through my eyes if I didn't make it through this alive. Steadying myself, I straightened my shoulders and lifted my chin.

"The Supernatural Council is hosting the first ever Mythic Games. The Mythic Games are a competition where teams from of any world can compete to demonstrate their magical strength and skill. All are welcome to the planning and the construction of the games, with the exception of those who will participate in the competition. Once a being is committed to the planning and building of the games, they will not be in contact with anyone until the games are completed. Agreeing to plan or compete means that all parties agree to the terms I've set. The Mythic Games will be broadcast throughout the multiverse, so all may witness the victory of the winning team. Please give your response as soon as possible. Those who do not respond in a timely manner, may not be accepted to compete in the games."

After I gave Athena a signal, she rubbed her hand over the owl's head. The bird condensed into a ball and then burst into a myriad of micro-owls. The smaller versions expanded to the size of the original, then the flock flew away and winked out of existence, passing from our world to their destinations. It was the same way we got all of the supernaturals organized to free the prisoners of the vault. I hoped they'd answer my call a second time.

"You have challenged the traitor," Hermes said, clasping a hand on my shoulder. "Creating new threads to the weave within the Tapestry of Fate to stop a devastating war. Be proud."

No pride manifested. It couldn't. My role wasn't over yet. The greatest challenge of my life lay ahead. Perhaps of all our lives.

I gave my lover and friend the biggest smile I could muster. Despite the effort I'd put into it, I doubted it was much of one. However, I wanted him to know how much I appreciated that he wanted to make me feel better. "Funny thing about pride. You have to had want to do something you're proud of in the first place to feel it." I gestured to where the owls winked out of the sky. "All I've done is sent a message."

"Fair enough." Hermes returned my grin with a full smile that reached his eyes. The caring in the depths of those brown eyes warmed some of the chill that had settled in my bones since the Moirai's bleak vision of the future.

There had been no whirlwind romance between us, not in the traditional courtship sense. Carlo had swept me off my feet, showing me an exciting life and then pulled the rug from under my feet to sweep someone else off theirs again and again. The moment I walked out of that figurative room with the same shabby rug, I thought I'd be on my own for the first time. The opposite was true.

Hermes showed up every single time I needed him, ready to aid or defend. I would do the same if something happened to him. We were a team. That was far more romantic to me than empty gestures and expensive gifts.

"There's something I'd like to do here," I said to the two gods.

Hermes took my hand. "We are in no hurry. Whatever you wish to do, I'll join you, my treasure."

Normally, that would be perfect. At the moment, I squeezed Hermes's hand. "Alone."

Hermes's brow furrowed, but Athena nodded. "I do as well."

She faced her brother. "Would you take me to my city?" With a glance in my direction, she added, "We are not in the council's jurisdiction and it would be wise to use every advantage we can get."

I shrugged. Supernatural council member or not, I couldn't care less about Gabriel's rules for the gods. Not when it came to Hermes and Athena, or anyone else for that matter. I wasn't there when the council was formed. I agreed to be a member because they'd been good allies. Also, as long as Lucinda remained in the Underworld, I wanted our pantheon to have a say.

After the gods left, I took a walk. With each step I let memories that weren't mine slip in and out. Usually, I kept the knowledge and memories of the other women who came before me out of my head and stored in a mental locker. Down the hill, among the ruins of temple and banks, I found the Navel and the Oracle stone. The Navel was a dome-like stone that was supposedly the navel of the entire world. The Oracle stone was what was left of the floor where the Oracles of ancient times held audiences. There was a groove where a channel had flowed with the noxious liquids that had provided vapors to help the Oracle go into a trance. Also, there were three holes where the Oracle's tripod dug deeply into the floor.

The whole space was a fraction the size of the temple where I served as Oracle in the Washington Olympic mountains. The Oracle's stone, so small for a person of such great importance to Greek kings, politicians, and generals alike.

I ran my fingers over the stone. A memory came to mind. Surprisingly, one of my own.

Papus wiped down the table after I refilled the napkin dispensers and salt and pepper shakers. We had a rhythm, working together in perfect harmony. Yiayia sang in the kitchen as she swept. Busy work my friends at school never had to do. But, most of them didn't even see their caregivers. Still, I wanted to go home. I had school in the morning and homework to do. Maybe papus would let me take the bus now and they could finish up closing duties without me.

"I have a social studies test tomorrow. I hope I get an A. It'll take a lot of studying." I made a big show of looking at my watch. I said "social studies" because I didn't want to say history. The first question that would

come out of his mouth would be "Who's history?" If I told him the Bronze Age, we'd be here until it was too late to study from my textbook.

His bushy eyebrows lifted. "What are social studies?"

When they first took me in, I used to think this made him look mean. It took very little time to learn papus was a gentle man with infinite patience for the American girl of his Apollonia.

However, I didn't want to share what I had to study because he would tell me a wild bedtime story, a fanciful fairytale filled with information that was never in any of the textbooks. I liked their stories well enough, but they were just that. Their own village's version of myths and history. I learned a long time ago not to use my grandparents' version of anything in school.

Papus grinned, still waiting for me to answer.

I blew out my breath. "History, I guess."

As predicted, his whole face lit up. "What period?"

After much study of my fingernails, I replied, "Bronze Age. Trojan War myth."

"That was no myth! Have I ever told you about the Trojan War? Our family was there! They played a part in how the gods affected the outcome. Very cunning business."

I grimaced. I hated when he acted like his stories were family history. "Helen of Troy and all that? Yeah."

My cheeks heated at the memory. I went by his version in seventh grade.

How could he forget? They were called in by the teacher. She'd advised them to get me a notebook because I was excellent at creative writing, but next time I had to write what was in the textbook and taught in class or I wouldn't get credit.

My grandfather nodded slowly. "I see. Well, I hope you remember what we've taught you. It might not get you an A on the test, but you'll need it one day."

Yiayia came out of the back, broom in hand. "It is your heritage, your history, and your culture. Whether American schools want to teach different." She shrugged a shoulder. "Doesn't matter to us Greeks."

Papus clasped my shoulder. "We are not senile. What we tell you is a history that has been passed down by elders to youth in preparation for the life they will lead. Remember all the players and the ways they influenced the gods. Remember the games and wars and all the little details. Without knowing your past, you will not be equipped with the knowledge you'll need in the future."

I blinked and I was back at the ruins, hand on the Oracle stone. They'd known all along that I would come to this moment. I regretted not appreciating it then. I would honor their memory by using the advantage they gave me.

CHAPTER

FIVE

The evening light limned Arachne's garden in gold. She, Athena, Nora, and Hestia weeded. Their light banter a soundtrack to my evening read on the back porch swing. One of Cerberus's three heads barked as the other two panted while he chased Greg. The spider expertly led the underworld pooch down the garden paths so they could play their game without trampling anything that would put Arachne into a tizzy.

The backdoor squeaked, alerting me to Hermes' presence. The god brought a tray carrying two iced teas.

"For my studious sweet potato."

"Thank you, my baby carrot." I took one of the glasses from the tray and gulped down the sweet, slightly fruity tea. It was just the refreshment I needed. "Post dinner sleepies averted."

He winged a dubious eyebrow.

"Alright. My carrot. There is nothing *baby* about you." I winked and waved the book. "Although, I must confess that I can't claim to be studious. I'm reading a cozy mystery novel, not a textbook."

Hermes set the tray on the porch and sat next to me with his own tea in hand. He nodded to the book. "I see there is a cat on the cover and a little cottage. That's different than the books you read for plea-sure before. Those had many shirtless, athletic men on the cover."

It was my turn to quirk an eyebrow. However, I doubted I appeared quite as cool as Hermes when he did it. When I packed to go out west, I hadn't taken any of my old romance novels with me. I'd figured I wouldn't need them to get me through loneliness like I needed them when I was married to Carlo. "How did you know I read those?"

"We'd lost so many Oracles to mysterious circumstances. Zeus wanted me to take no chances with you. Sometimes, I had to enter your home or watch you closely when Carlo made enemies. I stopped a few from attacking you. The fool believed he was lucky. I was his luck."

"What about watching me closely on that whole cross-country trip?"

He grimaced. "Zeus wanted his enemies to show themselves. The plan worked, but I *was* watching you, even then. I had to report back to Zeus before I could act."

Pain limned his handsome face as he stared down into his tea. Did he feel he failed me by doing as he was ordered? I was a blip in his life and his father had been there for eons. I held no grudge against him for what happened. God or not, Hermes had been a pawn in his father and brother's game just as I had been.

I tried to keep a straight face, but the corner of my mouth twitched as I asked, "Did you read any of the books?"

I almost teasingly added *stalker*, but he seemed to have a lot of shame around the subject. I don't know why. After taking a nosedive off a building, I would have been ground beef if he hadn't watched me. If the council hadn't rescued me, Hermes would've rescued me from the Titans.

The god's cheeks darkened.

Was that a blush?

"Not the ones from your home, I bought them."

Both of my eyebrows shot up. "Why?"

He shrugged and looked off to some unseen point. Then he closed his eyes and exhaled through his nostrils. "You fascinated me. There was this vibrant woman so full of life and heart, a bit of a trickster, but never in a way that hurt people. I wanted to know why you were devoted to someone like Carlo, someone who hurt people often and put you and your child in harm's way more times than I can count. If I hadn't been there-" He shook his head. "I just wanted to know what drove you to him."

"Do you think you found an answer in what I read?"

"Carlo was exciting, handsome, and charismatic, like an anti-heroes in your books. I may be a god and that might be exciting to some, but I am not someone to bring turmoil to you intentionally. I want a peaceful existence. A simple life with little weight on my shoulders is what I have always desired." With a long sigh, he also admitted. "I want to be a hero to you, better than the standard set in a fiction. Perhaps then, you would consider me someone worthy to marry."

I suddenly found the ice cubes in my tea very fascinating. Hermes admitted to a lot more than what was said, and he'd said a lot.

We sat in silence for a while. Cerberus and Greg tired out. The giant spider returned to his mother and the three-headed doofus loped onto the porch and settled on the floorboards in front of the porch swing. The others retired to the house.

"Want some chow?" Nora asked Cerberus, pausing at the door on her way in.

All three heads lifted. One head barked in answer. He followed her through the screen door, tail wagging.

The only ones left outside were the two of us and the big admission.

Hermes took my empty glass and made like he was going to go in as well.

I put a hand on his arm. The lightest of touches, but that was all it took to stop him.

"My mother abandoned me. My grandparents had loved me, but

they'd died. I had no connections to extended family in Greece, and no friends who were doing any better than I was. I had no one that had stuck around.

Carlo might have charmed a younger version of me, but I grew tired of his turmoil after Luke was born. No one else had ever stuck around long. Carlo did. How could I leave someone who stood by me?" I shrugged. "The thing was, he was never there. At least not mentally. You can live years with someone and be utterly alone. Sometimes people just do what's easy, what they know."

"I see. So, if you bore of me...as long as I stay, you will not leave me, at least not in body." His shoulders slumped.

"I'm never staying just to stay again. I wouldn't do that to you," I promised.

I gestured to him and myself. "I never dreamed of this. I didn't know what we have was even a possibility for someone like me. I thought what I had with Carlo was easy and safe, but it never was. It was nothing like the way I feel every day with you. "

I took the glasses out of his hands, set them on the tray he'd put aside, and I held his hands in mine.

"You've known who I was, who I am for a very long time, but I have known you for very little in comparison. What I do know is that you don't have to be my hero. You just must show up like you have again and again, spend time with my son, make me deliriously happy in all aspects—even when we're at odds. We only disagree about marriage. It's not a matter of your worthiness, but my readiness. I'm not ready to marry you, but I am in love with you, Hermes. I want a simple life with you in this little town with the friends and family we've made. Isn't that enough?"

My chest squeezed so tight I couldn't breathe when he let go of my hands. He stared at me with an unreadable look in his eyes. Then, ever so tenderly, he wiped my tears away with his thumbs. He kissed my forehead, my wet lashes, my cheeks, my nose and my chin. Then his lips found mine. The kiss was tender at first and then grew passionate, his arms pulling my body against his. I wrapped my arms around his torso, holding him with all I had, too.

Hermes didn't break our kiss when he stood, walked us through the Null and into our bedroom. There, he broke away to slide down my yoga pants and undies.

I lifted my shirt and took off my bra. As his dark eyes raked over my naked body, I felt beautiful, sexy, and powerful. The hunger that lurked in the depths of his gaze made my body ache to feed his desire and quench some of my own as the need to show him how much I felt built.

He sank to his knees before me.

My heart fluttered and a note of trepidation sang along with the building desire. Would he ask me to marry him again?

He answered the burning question of what he would do next with the dip of his head.

A gasp escaped my lips as he bit the tender flesh of my inner thigh. He'd never done that before. I was as surprised that he'd did it as I was at my body's reaction. I was slick with need, ready for more of wherever this was leading.

"Sorry, I should have given fair warning, but I couldn't help it," he whispered against my skin, placing a kiss where he'd sunk his teeth. His voice was almost a grow as he added, "Your thighs are so thick and scrumptious, I had to take a bite."

Panting, I replied, "Um, I liked it."

"Oh?" He did it again on the other side, sending heat and wetness straight to my center. "And that?"

"Yes."

Hermes played a little game of bite and kiss all over my thighs, over the indent of my hips, and belly. His hands roamed over my curves and cupped my breasts. A thumb circled my nipples, creating waves of pleasure that went directly to another sensitive bundle of nerves. It was too much and not enough. I didn't want it to end, but I also wanted him inside me. His skin against mine.

"Turn around and spread your legs."

Heart racing, I did as he asked.

"So fucking delectable," He whispered before biting the curve of my ass. He stood and gently pushed me until I was bent over the bed.

Anticipation licked my skin in electric tingles. Hermes laid a tender kiss on the nape of my neck and then painted a trail of them down my spine.

I could feel his hot breath on my sex right before he nuzzled his face right between legs, licking my lips before spreading them with his fingers. With my verbal encouragement, he took turns teasing my sensitive bundle of nerves with his lips and tongue and delving his tongue and fingers inside me. Like a tide of floodwater rising against a dam, the pressure before release built inside me. Until it broke, and I gushed all over him.

With no time to recover, Hermes was inside me. He made love at a frantic pace, as if branding himself into my flesh and bone, and very soul. Hitting a sweet spot until he brought me again and then spent himself.

It wasn't until we were sprawled on the bed did he say, "As long as you love me as you do in this moment, I would wait a thousand lifetimes for you to be ready."

I traced a lazy trail along the space between his pecs down his abdomen. "I don't think it will take that long."

A twinkle of mischief sparked in his dark eyes. "Was it that good?"

I snorted. "If I married you based on the sex, we'd have been married the first time."

In response, he looked very self-satisfied. "I learned much from your books."

Somehow, I doubted an ancient god learned from romance novels, but I laughed anyway. I was tired but not yet sleepy.

"Speaking of books, do you mind if I read a bit before we turn out the lights?" I got up to put on my robe.

He was gone and back before I could tie the belt. Book in hand and still naked. "You can read to me this cozy mystery, if you'd like."

"I'll have to start over from the beginning, or you'll be lost."

He bowed in mock acquiescence. "I appreciate your sacrifice."

"True. My charity knows no bounds."

We slipped back into bed, not bothering with nightclothes. I opened the book.

CHAPTER

SIX

Flags marked where the last three javelins woefully missed Athena's mark. I hefted the spear over my shoulder and positioned myself. Deep breath in. *You got this.* On the exhale, I threw with all my might.

This time, I only missed by a foot.

I spun around to look at Hermes. He grinned ear to ear, approval and pride in his eyes.

"Again," Athena ordered.

Sighing, I jogged to retrieve the javelin.

Arachne skittered over with a flag, marking the spot.

Back in position and ready to launch, I paused and looked to the opening ceiling. I was not the only one. All around the gymnasium, harpies, gods, nymphs, and all manner of supernaturals stopped what they were doing and looked up.

Nicky flew over to us, landing next to me. "The harpy scouts reported an incoming wave of Athena's messengers."

My gut clenched. We needed all the heavy hitters to say yes, or Apollo would grow bored. Growing bored meant he might still enact his plan. Zeus and the other gods drew near as a myriad of tiny owls descended from the open ceiling.

Athena held out her hand. The owls paused, hovering above us like a cloud. She spoke loudly so everyone could hear, "Before I play the formal responses. The white eyes are acceptance. The black eyes are a rejection to the invitation. I'll play the black-eyed owls first."

The goddess then made a gesture. Out of the extensive flock, only a few came back with black eyes. A few pantheons I'd not ever heard of made clear they had nothing to prove, and this world being destroyed didn't bother them in the least—it would actually be better that their former worshippers' descendants perished for abandoning them. So much for getting all their power from mundane humans. Perhaps they had decided ascending wasn't worth it. I didn't have the emotional capacity to care beyond Apollo's answer.

Six supernaturals dressed in fine furs, armor, and elaborate jewelry appeared in holographic form. They were seated at a long table with a wood beam ceiling above, skins of animals, shields, and axes decorated the wall above a mantle. Directly behind them, a fire roared in a colossal hearth. Upon the table, the hologram was so life-like, it felt like a window into another world. The magic and tech in Athena's owls were even wilder than some of the I.S.E.A agent gadgets.

Hermes, who had drawn close, whispered, "Asgardians."

I'd figured as much because at least one present had assisted with the Vault prison break. I believe he was Fenrir.

Odin's grandfatherly look seemed similar that of Zeus. His hair was longer, wavy, not curly. He wore several braids, and one side was shaved. He wore a patch over the eye he'd given up in Mimir's well—or so the legend went. Since becoming Oracle, I'd learned a lot of the human versions of stories were their understanding of what happened.

"We accept your challenge. Here are our terms. Brokkr, Eitri, and Sindri will be our game planning and construction representatives.

Our team will comprise of Freyja, Loki, Thor, Fenrir, my Valkyrie generals, and myself."

Odin made some stipulations. Mainly that his pantheon be allowed access to the Americas the fae enjoy.

I called Gabriel. Surprisingly, I got him right away. He'd given me his cell. That didn't always get me through to him. Sometimes I got Princess.

After getting over my initial shock, I explained the situation.

He cursed. After a brief pause, the were-nephil replied, "He won't be the first to ask. All access to this territory will be granted to everyone who competes after the games, but they will have to first go through a visa process just like the fae. Have him send me a raven for the details."

"Fun. I have to explain bureaucracy to a war god."

Gabriel chuckled. "Odin is reasonable." Before he hung up, he asked, "Did he really say he'd bring Loki?"

"Yeah."

A loud exhale later, he said, "Well, that's tomorrow's problem, isn't it?"

Since I didn't think he would explain why he thought the trickster was a problem, I made noise of affirmation.

After I hung up with Gabriel, we let another owl play. The next owl revealed High King Oberon of the Unseelie Court. Next to him were two more fae I didn't recognize, beautiful and as haughty in appearance as the pink haired, white antlered Oberon. To my surprise, the wolf shifter named Carmen had her arm linked with the king's. Carmen had worked quickly to become part of his royal entourage. Had Miriam made the right choice in picking her father's domain for the murderous shifter?

Oberon inclined his head. "I accept your invitation. I will give you access to two of my court architects for the building of the game. Princess Aoife and Prince Faigan of the Seelie court will join me to represent the high fae, as well as my bride to be, Carmen."

Her grin was wolfish as the animal she shifted into, and her dark eyes were so very, very off. I hoped Miriam would look out for her. Something told me Carmen wanted the throne.

We heard from a few lesser known to me pantheons. The next contender gave me the chills just to look at.

The king of Hell appeared. His body relaxed in a languid pose. His black wings the same shade as his long hair and eyes. He wore an obsidian silk robe that barely covered his sculpted, lethal form. He seemed to look straight at me, his gaze at once alluring and terrifying. "This should be amusing. I'm in. I'll send two demons and one of my lord engineers. My team, as you call it, will be comprised of the Princes of Hell, known in your world as the Fallen. If the angels do not agree to this competition, tell my brother Gabriel that I am personally competing. They will change their minds quickly. Also, relay to Tatiana, or Miriam as she calls herself these days, that she has a place here if that Olympian brat succeeds."

The image winked out. I rubbed my forehead. I would *not* be relaying the latter message. "Just how long does it take an immortal to realize it's over?" I muttered.

"Quite some time. Sometimes never." Hermes's expression seemed to speak from experience.

All my muscles ached from the tension coiling through my body. I felt as if I was going to faint from the extended suspense or perhaps sheer exhaustion? Either way, hours of standing and waiting while going through replies had taken a toll.

Zeus stepped forward. "Enough with this. I want to see Poseidon and Hades's replies, and then *his*."

Athena halted the next owl with a wave of her hand. Her eyebrows furrowed in concentration.

We all waited with bated breath.

A troubled expression marred Athena's face. "I cannot sense the one that I sent to Olympus, father."

I inhaled sharply. This whole competition didn't matter a lick if Apollo denied a response.

"Would you like to hear from the two kings?" Athena asked. She directed the question at me, not her father.

He replied anyway. "I would."

Her gaze shifted to me.

I nodded. At least we'd find out where Hades and Atlantis stood.

Two other owls separated from the flock. Poseidon's response owl projected a hologram of him in his throne room. New construction covered the area where Scylla had left a gaping hole. The rubble, the blood, the stone tentacles had all been cleared out, leaving no trace of the battle that could have destroyed Atlantis.

Next to Poseidon stood the admiral of the mighty Eel Navy and my erstwhile protector, Cosmo. There was also a naiad with blue skin and gills. She wore a warrior's armor. Also a melusina and a few more seamen from the Eel Navy, judging by their stance and weapons.

Poseidon's snowy eyebrows furrowed together. "I accept. I will send some of my best engineers for the planning and will have a team of Atlanteans join me." He blipped out with no stated additional terms.

Zeus let out a loud breath that sounded a lot like relief. Demeter touched his shoulder. He laid a hand over hers.

Had he worried his brother would keep out of it or did the former king of the gods worry Poseidon had sided with Apollo?

Hades appeared dark and gorgeous. He donned midnight armor. Persephone, dressed much the same, spoke, "My husband, Aidoneus Hades, and I, rulers of the Underworld accept your invitation. We will send our best engineers. Also, my husband and I will have sirens, harpies, Thanatos, and Melinoë on our team."

A few of the former Olympians gasped. All color drained from Hermes's face when Persephone announced Melonoë would come. Even Athena blanched. Demeter and Zeus exchanged furtive glances. Who was she? I'd heard her mentioned before, but the myths were different.

I didn't have time to contemplate why this person was so important before the next owl and subsequent holograph appeared.

Hermes was still as a statue. His jaw was tight and eyes fierce. It wasn't just us. No one gathered in the gymnasium seemed at ease.

It was hours before the final owl centered itself before me to relay its message. Several glowing persons in light colored tunics with gold belts faced me. Each had a pair of shimmering wings. I'd almost believe they were fae, if Oberon hadn't already appeared.

Also, Gabriel, the angel, looked a lot like Gabriel, the werenephil. He possessed a leaner body but did not appear older. In fact, this angel looked timelessly young, but there were eons in his eyes, just like his brother Lucifer.

"We accept. You'll receive two engineers. A team of four seraphim of our choosing will be our team."

The angels disappeared.

CHAPTER

SEVEN

The shower pelted my skin with liquid heat, loosening taut muscles and easing aching joints. Eyes closed, I let the water saturate and ease my mind as well as my body.

Letting go and acknowledging something is out of your control is difficult, to say the least. I had to do it so many times to stay married to Carlo. His destructive patterns of behavior had been part of who he had been, still was, and I'd had to accept that to stay married to him. Unlike many in the same situation, I'd never lied to myself. Instead, I developed a pattern of chipping away my pride and my dignity, letting go of it all in sacrifice to the altar of a peaceful home.

This time, the stakes didn't solely involve my marriage, my self-worth, and my wellbeing. So many lives hung in the balance. Apollo's actions would cause a ripple of damage throughout the entire multiverse. He didn't deserve godhood let alone ascension.

Funny, how I could save Atlantis, Milagro Bay, and now, I wanted to save everyone. That was easy. Claiming my own worth and at the same time de-centering myself in all of this? Not so much.

After the shower, I dressed to serve as Oracle, and went down-

43

stairs. One day a week, we didn't train. All of the gods would hear prayers, and I would hear petitions to tell people their future.

Arachne, Nicky, Athena, Hermes, and Nora were at the table. Cerberus munched on something in the corner of the room. One head lifted and made happy eyes and lolling tongue as he panted his greeting.

Hermes scooped something delicious smelling onto his plate as the other three chatted. His dark eyes caught sight of me. After a slow once over, he said, "Kalimera!"

Gregory scuttled up and circled my feet.

"Good morning to you, too." I grinned, waiting for the giant spider at my feet to get over that I wasn't going to cuddle him. Tolerating his presence might be all I would be ever capable of and he'd have to accept that.

"She's not going to pick you up, so quit trying, Greggy" Arachne chided, gently.

At one last ditch attempt at affection, *Greggy* tapped my foot.

I'd gotten better at controlling my reactions around Arachne's children, but a nervous squeak escaped my throat.

Cerberus stopped eating and whined in the spider's direction. Out of all of Arachne's children, the pooch loved Gregory the best.

Greg made a sound that would have been a sigh, if spiders could sigh, and then skittered over to Cerberus. The Underworld hound affectionately licked the top of the corgi-sized spider, and then went back to eating.

Gregory happily spun a bit and then shook like a wet dog, spraying slobber.

"Hey!" Nora's face screwed up in disgust as she wiped viscous liquid off her arm with a napkin.

Finished with herself, she looked at Athena, raising her napkin then pausing before actually touching her. "Um, goddess? You have a bit of that dog's ick in your hair."

"Oh, I'm aware. I can smell it." Athena cast an indignant look at the offender and then his mother, revealing that there was indeed a web of wet gunk netting the back of her head. As if to accentuate the point, some spittle dripped onto her shoulder.

The goddess kept her composure except for an involuntary shiver of revulsion.

Barely containing a laugh, Arachne shrugged. "Greg was just helping Cerberus spread the love."

"Instruct your child to shake the love elsewhere." Her gaze again swept to the offending pooch. "With three heads, thus thrice the mucous, Cerberus is quite capable of spreading his affections all on his own."

"Let me," Nora began, hovering with the napkin.

"No need." With an elegant flick of her hand the slobber disappeared from Athena's head and everywhere else it had landed.

TEMPLE MORNINGS PLAYED out differently now that Zeus and the other gods showed up to hear prayers. Thankfully, I didn't have them all in the temple where I served. Hephaestus erected additional buildings to serve as the gods. Even Hermes had a temple. Pilgrims flocked to the gods in even greater numbers than I'd ever seen as Oracle.

It was quite the spectacle. We had harpies and some sirens lent from Persephone to handle the crowds outside, priestesses like Nora and Arachne handled the petitioners inside. Those who had ideas about testing the mortality of a god, quickly lost their gumption in the face of Zeus and the earthbound remnants of the Twelve. However, I kept two harpy guards, including my mom, Nicky. Arachne and Cerberus were extra protection.

With the Big Wigs around, I'd thought no one would come to see me anymore. I'd been wrong. Even in a time when you could make a personal request from a god, people still sought their future. What can I say? One was like taking a chance on someone saying they'd make it rain for you. The other was like looking through the window and seeing if storm clouds were gathering. Neither was for certain, but my money was on the clouds.

Cerberus in his black Labrador glamour lay at my feet as I sat upon my tripod set upon a dais. He didn't need to keep up the glamour for disguise purposes anymore, but the petitioners had less trouble speaking when there wasn't a three-headed monster in front of them.

A big man in his forties, judging by the gray in his auburn hair and middle-aged thickening in the waist and broadening of his shoulders, approached. He was accompanied by a woman, slightly smaller in stature, also graying and a few lines touched her forehead and around her mouth. The placement of her wrinkles told me she worried a lot.

Between them in the center, they each had a hand on a teenager about sixteen or seventeen. She had a mixture of her parents features and her father's auburn hair. The teenager was pretty, but not in the way all young people were. She had a extraordinary features, but she didn't possess the freshness of youth. Dark circles haunted her eyes and her hair appeared slightly disheveled, as if she were a mother of two small children and didn't get much sleep, not a kid on the cusp of adulthood.

My heart sank. Normally, we didn't allow children, or more than one person at a time, but this was obviously a special case. These people were no security threat.

The girl grinned at Cerberus's languid form. Her gaze then darted to Arachne. Apprehension slowed her steps.

I'd grown used to my friend's appearance, forgetting her affect upon mundane humans.

The top half of Arachne's body seemed normal enough. Nothing is frightening about a bespectacled, thin, elderly woman. Her eyes were kind and her smile warm as the sun. However, Arachne's lower body was disproportionately larger than her torso, rounder than a human's body, but not quite a perfect sphere. Not much showed through her opaque, floor length chiton. Probably a bit of glamour or illusion magic obscured what was happening underneath. Other than her eight spider legs I'd caught glimpses of, even I didn't know. I made it a point to never think about where and how she stored her army of corgi-sized spider children under her skirts.

Even with an illusion, something about Arachne's proportions triggered the flight or fight instinct in mundanes. Emphasis on the flight.

The parents huddled closer to their daughter. Their trepidation seemed to have the opposite effect than her initial reaction, bolstering the girl. She lifted her chin, proceeding forward with a confident stride. Her parents also picked up the pace.

Arachne held out a collection plate. I shook my head, indicating I didn't want a tithe for this one. Without reading her thread, I knew this family was eyeballs deep in medical bills and wanted to know how long they had with her.

The girl made a little curtsey and dipped her head. Her blue gaze then met mine, unafraid. However, her throat bobbed before she repeated the words learn by rote followed by her own question, "Oh Oracle, I beseech you. How long will the remission last?"

I knew a question of the sort was coming, but it didn't prepare me for the way her words wound around my mother's heart. We could all die, if Apollo had his way. But the god's machinations were so far removed from the personal crucible this young woman and her parents were enduring.

"Come here. I must touch you, to read your thread." I held out my hand.

She licked her lips. A little of her former confidence wavered. Glancing at her parents, she stepped onto the dais, and put her cold, thin hand in mine.

My Oracle gift now a part of me and well-practiced, I no longer separated myself between my ability, and my conscious self.

"Would you like to know the amount of time or all the wonderful things you'll do in that time?"

The girl's mouth twisted as she deliberated the question. Behind her, a tear streamed down her mother's cheek. She quickly wiped it away. Her father opened his mouth to speak.

Arachne put a finger to her lips.

Like the mother, I wanted to cry. Like the father, I wanted to protest. The injustice of someone so young never living out the summer and winter of her life hurt. I wanted to fix it.

For a moment, the young woman looked much older than someone her age. It wasn't in her appearance, but the type of acceptance and self-fortifying attitude an adult must muster when faced with only bad options.

"Tell me what I will do—er." As if she remembered what the harpies outside told her to do and say, she bowed her head and petitioned. "Oh, Oracle, will you grant me your wisdom and tell me of the things that I will experience?"

Braids of thorns wrapped around my chest and squeezed. I swallowed the lump forming in my throat. "I will. However, I won't share details like names and specifics that will spoil the moments."

She nodded that she understood.

"You will visit an ancient city."

The girl's forehead wrinkled in confusion.

"A school trip with all of your friends. There, you will buy a souvenir that will shock your teacher and mother but make your father laugh."

She giggled behind her hand. Her parents exchanged a look.

"You will dance under twinkling lights, bass reverberating through your body. You will feel beautiful, freer and lighter than you ever have, as if you could reach the heavens."

Her eyes shone and she had a faraway look, as if imagining this dance. Her parents exchanged rueful grins and held hands. Their eyes misted with tears as they listened.

"You will curl your toes in warm sand under a cerulean sky, the crash of waves in your ears and the smell of brine heavy in the air."

With a dreamy look in her eyes, she sighed.

"Your first kiss will be a big disappointment, but your second will make your heart soar and your head spin."

With her free hand, she touched her chest. Behind her, the mother laid her head on the father's shoulder.

"You will know what it's like to love and be loved." I squeezed her hand before letting go. "That is all I may share."

She grinned ear to ear. "Thank you."

Her parents dried their eyes and nodded their thanks.

I turned to Arachne and told her in Greek, "Walk them out and tell the harpies at the door to give me a minute before the next petitioner."

She did as I bid. As soon as they were out of the temple and earshot, I let the tears go.

Soon, Arachne laid a gentle hand on my back. "How long does she have?"

I looked up. I swallowed down the next wave of tears and managed to speak. "She'll die peacefully in her sleep tonight."

"Shouldn't we warn her parents?" I shook my head. "They know. I could see it in their eyes as I lied."

"Huh. Why would they go through such trouble to get her here for a lie?'

"It was her dying wish. I figure they'd brought her to me, hoping I would tell her something she wanted to hear. A future that would have happened if her body didn't give out on her. She will die dreaming of her crush, dancing, and curling her toes in the sand."

Arachne squeezed my shoulder. "In a way, I'm jealous of her."

I cocked my head to take in her face. "How so?"

"She'll go peacefully. I fear I won't. I fear that many of us will still lose our lives and this game will not occur."

There was one way to find out. I could examine the threads. Everyone knew I could see whether the war would happen or not, but I had promised I wouldn't. That was a stipulation of the games many of the other pantheons made.

"I also fear these games won't be peaceful. I can feel it in my old bones and carapace that Apollo and some others will fight dirty. This will not be a friendly competition."

I had only considered the loss of life on Earth being minimized. I hadn't even begun to contemplate foul play during the games and who I might lose.

"You don't have to participate." Luke wasn't, not directly. He was picked by I.S.E.A to monitor the games, but he would not put himself in direct danger. I at least had that.

"I have committed to being your friend, your protector, and serving at your side. That means being there for your darkest hour."

I got up and wrapped my arms around my friend's thin shoulders. I'd never had an aunt, but Arachne filled that role and I was grateful.

"I love you."

Arachne squeezed me back and stroked my hair. "I love you, too, sweet Lydia. I love you, too."

CHAPTER

EIGHT

A knock at my bedroom door woke me. Hermes dressed and answered, before I could wipe the sleep out of my eyes. On the nightstand, my phone's screen read that it was five in the morning. I groaned. There was still an hour until my alarm would go off. With all the training, I coveted every second of rest.

Hermes turned, apology in his handsome features. "Nora would like to speak to you."

Knowing Nora wouldn't wake me unless it was urgent. I rose and wrapped a bathrobe around me, belting it by the time I reached the door. I managed a sleepy grin. "Everything okay?"

Her pretty face, now fuller from regular meals and rested from the sleep one gets in permanent housing, grinned shyly. "Yeah. Sorry. I need your counsel."

I kissed Hermes on the cheek. "Go back to bed, my love."

Not much later, Nora and I were tucked away in my front office, steaming cups of coffee in our hands. We didn't talk at all in the meantime. I sensed she'd come to me reluctantly and without her chosen goddess's knowledge since Athena was the person Nora went

51

to for advice and it was an hour before Athena rose. The priestess stared at the mug in her hands but didn't drink.

Understanding she needed some prompting, I said, "What do you need counsel on."

"I wish to compete."

I paused mid sip and stared at her. "You're a mundane."

The priestess clasped her chest and gasped. "I am? Well, that's news to me. I thought I was a unicorn."

Chuckling, I waved away her comment. "Alright, I deserved that. My point is that this is a competition for supernaturals."

Nora tapped her chin. "Isn't mundane belief behind the magic of all supernaturals?"

"It's more like a power boost." I was hedging and we both knew it.

She leaned toward me, her face eager. "If that's so, my belief is important in these games. I can help."

I licked my lips, unsure of what to say. "You'll need a team."

She met my gaze. "Who's on your team?"

"The Supernatural Council, the harpies and witches of Milagro Bay, Hermes, Arachne, Zeus, and Athena."

"Athena, Arachne, Zeus, and Hermes aren't from Earth. Why are they representing Earth?"

"Arachne has lived on Earth longer than anyone alive. She is a resident," I corrected. "As for the rest, they have permanent residence visas recognized by the UN and the United States. Hermes has applied for Earth citizenship."

"Still, I want to represent humans and give you all a power boost in the games. It's my world that's up for grabs. Imperfect as it is, this is it for me. No refuge on another planet. Consider me for your team. That's all I ask."

"Nike Nora Jones, I will consider you for my team," I promised. The magic of it settling on my skin, binding me to my word.

Nora's eyes widened as she felt it. Finding her words after a few seconds of shocked awe, she said, "Thank you." Then the priestess rose. Hand on the doorknob, she turned her face in my direction. "You're who you were when I met you, kind and generous, but you've changed. However, you're also different than who she was. She felt normal, like anyone else on the street. Now, your energy crackles around you the way it does around the gods and other powerful supernaturals. Belief has affected your magic."

I swallowed hard. All the petitioners I'd seen. The viral content. It had changed me. Even Zeus said I was something of this world and something of his, something entirely new. More importantly, *I* felt the difference. Managing a grateful smile, I replied, "I know. I won't let it get to my head."

Nora turned fully so that her whole body faced me. She shook her head, long locks swaying with the movement. "No. Let it get to your head. You need to acknowledge you're no longer the underdog. You call the shots of this game. Be the powerful being you've become, not Francine. The weak parts of her are gone. The one who loved someone who didn't deserve it. The one who didn't know her worth. Lydia Kourakos is a match for Apollo both in power and understanding of your place in the multiverse."

My lip quivered as I thanked her for her confidence in me. Intellectually, I knew I was no longer the woman I'd been, but Francine Lawless would always be a part of me. Because there was one thing about Francine, and every name I'd gone by over the years, that nothing would take away. I was a resilient survivor, cunning as any god from day one. I would use those skills I'd honed against Apollo, a god who hadn't ever had to struggle for his next meal or anything at all.

Nora knew survival, too. She deserved to fight for her world. Besides, the cunning part of me knew I would need her advice and belief. I decided then she'd be on the team. Now to convince the others it was necessary.

～

THE SUPERNATURAL COUNCIL, the Milagro Bay harpies and witches, some of the council's friends and shifters were also practicing. Team Earth was big, but the games might be as well.

"I have an announcement," I said to anyone who would listen in the gymnasium.

Heads from all groups turned.

"Nike Nora Jones will be joining us as a mundane human. She will be there for support and for wherever Athena—" I nodded to the goddess. "—sees fit to place her."

Athena's gaze swept from me to her priestess. Her eyes narrowed. The goddess of wisdom didn't like surprises—especially when she was in charge of coordinating who would be on what team and I threw in a mid-prepping pick.

The apple of Nora's throat bobbed, but she kept her chin up.

"Join Arachne," Athena commanded.

Once everyone got back to business, the goddess strode to me. "If anything happens to her—"

I held up my hand, interrupting her. "No. No threats."

Athena blinked, shocked that I'd spoken to her as an equal. Tough titties. She was no longer a ruler of Olympus and I wasn't her priestess. Powerful being or not, she had no right to expect me to cower because I said something that pissed her off.

"Nora is not a child. She made the choice to represent her world. She bears the consequences."

Emotions warred on the goddess's beautiful features, until settling to serene acceptance. Athena gestured to our usual practice space. "Hopefully your aim with javelin will be as accurate as your admonition."

I suppressed a chuckle. "From your lips to the javelin's tip."

HARPIES AND WITCHES gathered around a sparring sand pit in Nicky's gymnasium. Miriam and Phyr, who had been practicing some sort of wild Unseelie battle magic, joined them. So did Princess and the shifters. Soon everyone in the gym gathered. Athena and I also paused our javelin tossing to see what was up.

In the center of the sand pit, Hermes and Gabriel sparred. Wings out, shirts off, sweat glistening on muscled arms and torsos, they didn't seem to notice the gathering crowd.

My heart lurched when I realized they weren't using practice weapons.

The god and the shifter-nephil moved at incredible speeds. Gabriel thrusted a sword. Hermes blocked with a shield and spun away. Sand sprayed in the wake. Well matched, sword clamored against sword, or was blocked by a shield. The fight took to the air, creating a swirling tornado of sand.

The gathered crowd stepped back. Giving them space as magic thrummed in the air.

Concerned this was going too far, I took a step forward. Phyr blocked my path. "This isn't about you."

"The heck it isn't. That's my-my consort." The word sounded silly, but we weren't married or even engaged and boyfriend was seemed juvenile and an inept description.

"Excepting a small skirmish or two, Gabriel has not done battle for a long time. Lucifer will attempt to slay him in the games."

Focused on their glowing eyes and weapons, I argued, "They're using real swords and magic."

Phyr drew my gaze to his amber eyes. "As will their enemies. This is intentional. They are both worthy opponents. Hermes has his own magical defenses. Your lover is no mere mortal who injures easily and heals slowly. He knows what he is capable of, and they both need practice with their, as you say, gloves off."

"Friendly fire," Miriam shouted and Phyr spun. The Unseelie prince and halfling held up their hands. With my harpy vision, I could see green light forming a barrier between us and a stray stream of golden white magic.

"Stop!" Miriam shouted, magic amplifying her voice.

A strong compulsion pelted my skin but didn't make it through my harpy defenses.

Thankfully, the fighting above ended abruptly.

Hermes and Gabriel landed. Magenta and golden white magic crackled around each, respectively. Their eyes still glowed with their power.

"Dudes, dim the high beams," Rhiannon shouted from among the witches. "We're all friends here."

A few nervous chuckles escaped the gathered crowd.

The two supernatural men took a few tense moments to shake off their battle lust and return to their neutral forms. With the threat gone, the barrier dissolved.

"Well met. I'm honored to spar with a warrior of your caliber." Hermes offered his hand.

Gabriel clasped it, smiling. "Thanks for not holding back. Not having met my match in a while, I needed the reminder."

Hermes grinned, but it didn't reach his eyes. Gabriel didn't notice. He went off to talk to Miriam and Phyr.

Hermes made his way to me.

"You held back?' I kept my voice barely above a whisper to avoid being heard by supernatural ears. It was loud with chatter in the gymnasium now that the show was over, but one couldn't be too careful in matters of pride.

The god grinned and put an arm around me, steering me away from the others. In a nearby alcove, he bit his bottom lip and looked over his shoulder, and then leaned in close enough I could smell the cooling sweat on his skin and the residual scent of his magic. "I gave Gabriel just enough fight to be a challenge. I started using magic when I realized he has no idea how powerful he has become since gaining fame, and he lost control more than once. I held back in that I was doing more protecting than true fighting."

My eyebrows furrowed. "Shouldn't you talk to him about this? What if he loses control in a fight against his real enemies and you aren't there to stop him from causing collateral damage?"

Hermes licked his lips, drawing my attention to his mouth. "I let one of his strikes go so that the people he'll listen to will talk to him."

"Phyr believed he needed to fight you."

He grunted. "He needed to—how do you say? —let off some steam. Having no control over this, to let you lead, instead of protecting you, it eats at him. He's used to being the shield between this world and other forces."

I grimaced in Gabriel's direction and then turned my attention back to Hermes' dark gaze. "I got that when he gave himself up to I.S.E.A. He's the kind of leader that will throw himself in front of others but would never allow anyone else to do so."

Hermes grinned. "I know someone else like that."

Rearing my head, I replied, "You're not like that."

Hermes cupped my cheek, his gaze darkening with something familiar. Still, the look made butterflies dance in my stomach. He pressed his forehead into mine.

"You, Lydia. I was talking about you, my harpy queen."

I almost argued that I was not the type to stick my neck out for anyone, but that wasn't true. Not anymore. The moment I realized Scylla would destroy Atlantis, I decided to stop running, stop letting things happen to me and take control of my place in things, I had thrown myself between the world and danger.

Warmth glowed within me, spreading to my limbs. Being seen when you sometimes didn't even see yourself fueled that warmth. Meeting his loving gaze filled with that sensation, I wrapped my arms around his neck and drew him to me.

I kissed Hermes with all the tenderness and affection I felt for him, the gratitude for knowing me as I truly was, and accepting and loving me.

He returned the kiss with equal feeling, enveloping me in his arms.

I broke the kiss because I had something important to say. "July Fourteenth, next year."

His eyebrows knitted and he tilted his head to the side. "What?"

"Our wedding. I'll marry you next year."

A little voice in the back of my head, whispered, *"If we survive this."*

Hermes let out a whoop of delight and crushed me against his chest, lifting me off the ground and spinning around. Half dizzy, I squealed, ignoring the naysaying niggling voice.

We left the alcove to announce to everyone the happy news. Hermes grinned ear to ear and I felt like I was floating on air. Finally, something to look forward to other than this damned competition.

Before we could make the announcement, a golden bird swooped into the gymnasium. My heart lurched. Athena's missing owl, the one we'd been waiting for from Apollo, had arrived.

CHAPTER
NINE

The owl projected the dais of the Twelve. Gods that I'd never seen before filled the thrones of the usual suspects. Apollo sat at the center, handsome and regal—no bored strumming of his lyre. Though, the instrument did remain at his feet. To his left were his mother, Leto, then Hera, Artemis, Ares, Aphrodite, and Adonis. To his right were unfamiliar faces.

Cronus, I decided, was to his immediate right. The Titan was larger than the others, likely eight or nine feet tall standing. The ancient god possessed a handsome face. Uncannily his features like that of Hermes and Zeus but without the warmth of the first or the fatherly look of the latter. Glacial was too warm of a descriptor for his gaze. Another factor differentiated the Titan from his son and grandson. Scars carved deep craggy ravines on his exposed skin. I shuddered at the sight of Zeus's handiwork. How could Hera stand for this? Excepting Zeus, Cronus had eaten and vomited his children. Did her contempt for her former husband outweigh the way their father treated them?

Like Louis the IV of France, Apollo seemed like a king who

indulged himself and often. Uranus seemed like a tyrannical warlord who humored the other as a public face.

"Oh, child. You walked upon the soil that so many paid homage to me and asked your ancestors to beseech me and that truly touched a place in my heart. If I had my way, the whole world would again seek you to hear from me." Apollo sighed. "Unfortunately, you allowed the Usurper and his traitorous son to poison you against me and your kin." He gestured to the Titans and the gods. "Your own grandmother tried to warn you."

I exchanged a look with Hermes. Apollo had gone completely delusional. Thanatos had said Dione had nothing to do with Apollo's plans. Dione herself had told them Apollo wanted to free the prisoners of the Vault. She never warned her against Zeus and Hermes.

My heart skittered as Dione stepped from behind Apollo's throne, positioning herself between the god and the Titan Cronus. Insidious whispers implied that I only had Hermes and Thanatos's word for what she'd said. If she hadn't been with Apollo all along, why was she there now? Did she lie to them, or did they lie to me?

"I don't blame my father and brother for what they've done, though. You see," Apollo continued, "the Moirai have been plotting against us gods for a very long time, poisoning their minds. Setting son against father over and over again. Why? Because the primordial gods made three weavers into the personifications of Fate for their purposes. It was an egregious act, for certain, but not worse than the irreparable damage they've caused."

In the wake of this revelation, the silence in the gymnasium was a palpable thing. No one refuting his claims allowed doubt to creep into my heart. Were we all victims of a greater plot? Were the Moirai truly deceiving everyone as revenge?

Cronus's father was dead, murdered by his hand as prophesied he would do. He ate his children to prevent his own prophesied death. The first Titanomachy was fought as a result. The gods always listened to the Oracles. They believed every prophecy as set in stone. Phyr said that was not how the fabric of the universe worked.

I mentally shook my head. No. I'd seen what Apollo had done to my ancestors. I saw the war he wanted to wage. I saw what he did to my mother, to Thetis and her revenge, and how Amphitrite betrayed his plan and made one of her own. I saw with my own eyes his surprise when the undead naiads descended upon Olympus to stop him. There was no way the Fates could manipulate that. He was playing a long game here. I was certain of it.

"Since the Fates can see all, I had to be devious with my plans and play the villain, fully intending to overthrow Olympus. All the while having a secret plan to free my relatives and tell them what I've learned. So that we could find three more with the sight to replace the treacherous Moirai. This time, we need three volunteers. Dione has already accepted the mantle. Even now, I know you question my motives, so I know you won't be willing. Luke was left in the battle to free the Titans, so he likely believes I abandoned him, but I hadn't—evidenced by Dione's appearance near the gates of Tartarus."

He smiled ruefully. "So, I propose this. I, and the gods of my choosing, will compete in these games of yours. Only if you and Luke will agree to replace the current Moirai after the games."

There it was. The motivation for his lies. I'd suspected that he wanted something of the three remaining Oracles, and here it was. Controlling Fate would give him ultimate power.

"If you don't agree, I will have to bear the burden of murdering the Moirai and leaving them with no replacement. I will not show up to these games and neither will any of those you see before you."

My whole body went cold. I couldn't move, couldn't blink, couldn't breathe.

I could hear what he didn't say. Apollo and the Titans would do exactly as they pleased while the rest of the most powerful entities in the multiverse were in a prison of *my* making.

"WE HAVE TO ACCEPT HIS TERMS," I said, bleakly to Luke, I.S.E.A. agents Roanhorse, Tan, and Doyle, and the earthbound Olympians as well as those who had already gathered in Nicky's gymnasium.

My son shielded his face with his hands.

The decision was difficult for me, no one wants to be sealed away in a realm forever as an incarnation of a concept, especially at the price of the death of the original Moirai, but I was older. I'd had a life. Albeit, it felt in some ways it had just started when I became Oracle. However, whether I felt like I'd just began living or not, I had had a family and done many things in the last few years to be proud of. Luke was essentially still a newlywed, and hadn't had a chance to live into his golden years with Juan, let alone establish himself in his new career with I.S.E.A.

Luke lifted his head. His eyes were red around the rims and glistening with unshed tears. "Alright. If this will stop him from killing countless people, I'm in."

"Then we will answer his demands." Taking a deep breath, I added, "However, we will counter with terms of our own. We will agree to becoming the fates, but Apollo must not only participate in these games, but win. I'm not risking our future and all he has to do is show up."

To my surprise, I saw several nods from the Supernatural Council and I.S.E.A agents.

"I concur. This is a wise course of action," Athena said loudly enough for everyone to hear. That was enough for the uneasy Olympians. Most of the Olympians.

Hermes only stood at the side with his arms crossed.

Agent Tan stepped forward. Her gaze on me, then sweeping the rest of us gathered. "Thank you for including I.S.E.A in this plan. Every nation will still have their defense departments on high alert. This might be stalling. He may still attack."

I didn't argue that gods were bound by their word. Swearing to do something and not fulfilling it had a magical price. If I were in

Tan's position, I wouldn't trust someone else to protect my world either.

CHAPTER

TEN

Hermes remained quiet during the rest of the meeting, during the recording Athena had sent back to Apollo, and on the way back to the house. The household ate dinner in silence, all lost in their thoughts. Luke appeared tired and more world weary than when we summoned him. Juan wept silently as he robotically lifted his fork and shoveled food in his mouth. Now and then he glared in my direction. It hurt, but I knew none of this was my fault. I didn't fault him for blaming me. He couldn't glare at Apollo, so I got the brunt of his feelings.

My son took his husband's hand and squeezed. Juan dropped his fork and sobbed.

"We need some time alone." Luke announced, and the couple retired to their old guest room.

I couldn't blame them for not wanting to stick around. Judging from the storms brewing in Hermes's eyes as he rose from the table, he wasn't happy with me either. I watched him bus his plate and utensils to the kitchen with a heavy heart.

I didn't like myself either right now or what I offered to sacrifice.

Arachne got up. "I'll talk to him."

Exhausted from her first day of training, Nora excused herself, which only left Athena and myself.

The goddess placed her fork on the table and directed her gaze to me. "You must kill my brother."

I blinked, wondering if she was making a joke and when did she develop dark humor. After a moment, I realized she'd meant Apollo, not Hermes, and exhaled with relief. "Care to elaborate?"

"In any future where the gods all die, it's because they war. The obvious choice is for you to kill him. The Moirai are caretakers, they cannot manipulate the threads. If he wants to replace them, he believes he can control something that just *is*. There is no logic behind his thinking."

I wasn't too happy with Apollo, but premeditated murder? He didn't act alone. Where would the killing end? "What about those who support him?"

"All must be dealt with as well. The Titans weren't just warring against us over a prophecy. Cronus and the others..." A tear slid down her cheeks and her shoulders heaved with a shuddering sigh. Athena swallowed hard. "Sometimes immortals, especially gods who do not ascend after eons upon eons of existence, fall ill. It is an illness of the mind. They forget things at first. Then, they develop paranoia. Those suffering from this illness become suspicious of friends, family, lovers—it doesn't matter how close they are to the person. They invent intricate machinations against them that they must counter." She looked at her hands. "Cronus is my grandfather. The others are my kin. I don't want to harm them but banishing them to a realm where they can't harm anyone didn't work."

An idea burst to life, like a spring bursting from the ground. "What if we found a way to trap them in the Vault?"

"I've thought of that."

I cut her a sharp look. "Perhaps lead with trap instead of kill?"

"Everyone would have to be in agreement. Also, the trap would have to be a secret kept to a few outside those who build it. I've looked at this solution several ways. There's a good chance Apollo might have a traitor among us, who will make him privy to our scheme. I'm not sure Hephaestus isn't in league with him." She rubbed her temples. "Also, Dione will be able to see the betrayal. She'll warn him."

"This is all theoretical for now." I tapped my fork on the table, thinking. "We will need a trap for them, but also to keep from Dione from seeing that he'll be trapped."

Athena shook her head. "Impossible."

"Not impossible," Hermes said from the doorway. "But very unlikely. Unless..."

"Not her." Athena's lip quivered and her voice trembled.

"She's been chosen for Persephone and Hades' team. She's the only one who has no thread. Even the Moirai themselves can't see her."

This person piqued my curiosity. "Why would anyone not have a thread in the tapestry of life?"

As if chilled by a breeze, Athena rubbed her goose pimpled arms and ignored my question. "You of all people should stay away from her."

An expression I've never seen before passed over Hermes's face. His eyes had something akin to guilt brewing in them.

Why guilt?

Turning his focus back to his sister, he argued in a soft voice, "She'll listen to me."

"At what cost, Hermes?"

Sick of them not naming the person, I asked outright, "Can someone please let me in on who we're talking about?"

Hermes looked absolutely miserable. "Melinoë. Sometimes, she is Macria."

The same goddess everyone feared. My grandparents didn't tell me much about her. In hindsight, her name might have come up once.

"What is she the goddess of?"

"Nightmares, hauntings, ghosts...things better left unsaid.

Things no one else wants to take part in, she revels in." Athena's tone carried no small amount of disdain. "She's become what we all knew she would."

Hermes's scowl deepened the more his sister spoke. "Don't judge too harshly. We all had responsibilities thrust on us that became our nature."

Athena sniffed, her distaste for Melinoë saturating the goddess's sculpted features. "She was born of deceit and lives in the shadows. I don't trust her."

With the intense emotions bouncing around the room, I knew if I didn't bring the conversation back it would be lost in their petty disagreement. "What other choice do we have?"

The two gods remained silent for what seemed like an eternity but was likely a minute at most. Athena exhaled loudly and stood.

She removed her owl. "Don't go to Hades directly. Use this."

Hermes nodded, silently accepting Athena's owl. He gave me a mournful look before excusing himself to make his recording in private.

"This plan will end up in one or both of my brothers' demise. She'll listen to Hermes because she will do anything to feed on his unrequited love for her. Let's hope she has found a new toy," Athena announced, leaving the room.

A wound, one I'd thought had scarred over since I'd gotten over Carlo, cracked a little. It hurt the way it hurts when you see an old friend or lover that you'd had words with and were no longer speaking to.

THE DIGITAL CLOCK on the nightstand read 11:08 when Hermes quietly entered the room. I didn't think I could sleep, but exhaustion from the day had consumed me.

The god sat on the edge of the bed, the mattress depressing with his weight.

"Hey." I rubbed my bleary eyes.

"I apologize. I didn't mean to wake you. Go back to sleep, Lydia."

How many times had I heard that in my marriage? I gave myself a mental shake. Hermes wasn't my ex. I wasn't the same person either. We could talk about it.

"Athena said that you were in love with Melinoë."

"She shouldn't have told a story that wasn't hers."

The anger in his voice split the wound a little more. Carlo would get angry if people snitched on his doings. I waited for him to blow up. Again, Hermes proved he wasn't Carlo.

His shoulders deflated. "It was a long time ago. It was why I stopped being psychopomp and tricked Thanatos out of it. I wanted to go nowhere near the realm she inhabits."

He hadn't been psychopomp for roughly two thousand Earth years. He wasn't kidding about a long time ago. A niggling voice whispered, *"What was two thousand years to an immortal?"*

Hermes turned and reached for me, he cupped my cheek. "I will never keep you guessing where my heart lies. I vow to you, my heart is with you and will remain with you until you don't want it anymore."

That was it. Wasn't it? When you loved, you had a vulnerable bit of yourself in the hands of the other. It wasn't where you placed your happiness. That came from within. Part of love was trusting someone wouldn't throw away that vulnerable bit. If I was going to survive this and marry Hermes, I had to mend that wound for good and tell the niggling voice it was a liar.

"I believe you. I trust you with my heart, too, Hermes."

A smile lit his handsome face as he leaned in and showed me exactly how much he appreciated me saying that.

CHAPTER

ELEVEN

can now tell you from experience that the last thing you wanted to see when you opened your eyes was a hooded figure with a scythe swaying at the foot of your bed.

I bolted upright, clutching the sheet to my bare chest. "What the Hell are you doing in my bedroom?"

Before the intruder could answer, Hermes shot out of the adjoining bathroom stark naked. A toothbrush raised in a threatening position—likely a fraction of a second away from stabbing the intruder. Recognition lit in his eyes.

The hood swung toward Hermes and then back to me. A low chuckle that sounded like bones scraping together escaped the hood as Thanatos bent over.

The God of Death had the giggles.

Hermes lowered the toothbrush, but I could tell by the tightening of his jaw that he was still close to bludgeoning the other god for completely different reasons than being an intruder. We exchanged glances.

Sobering, Thanatos regained his composure. Barely. "Don't they have material to sleep in on this world or are you all going back to

69

when you ran around naked?" The voice from under the shadows of the hood sounded akin to a raspy shuffling of paper, still, his amusement came through loud and clear.

Hermes and I glared.

Thanatos threw up a bony hand in a half shrug. "What? Fashion trends are so fast here, I can hardly keep up. Should I undress?"

The toothbrush returned to a menacing angle.

Uh oh.

Before Hermes bludgeoned Death—well—to death, I decided to take the situation into my hands. "You're obviously here with us for a reason. Go wait for us outside my office downstairs."

He sketched a bow, disappearing with a wave of his scythe.

Hermes grimaced at the space where Thanatos stood. "I think I know why he's here."

Fifteen minutes later, Thanatos, Hermes, and I sat *fully dressed* in the comfort and privacy of my office.

The God of Death took on his human form, donning a black tuxedo with a bowtie.

Someone had seen "Meet Joe Black," I thought.

Thanatos cleared his throat. "The owl made its way to Melinoë."

Hermes' throat bobbed. My own heart skittered. We needed her, but I didn't know what she'd ask for in return.

He then pulled something seemingly out of thin air. He opened his large, thin fingers, releasing shimmering, gold dust onto my coffee table. Among the dust there were tiny pieces of metal flakes.

"Why did she destroy the owl?" I asked.

Thanatos's voice changed, softening and feminizing when he relayed what was obviously Melinoë's reply, "Tell Hermes, 'I shall take no side.'" The tone changed. "Also tell him that if he wishes to sway me, to stop sending me his ice queen of a sister's trinkets and to come to me and beg in his particular way, I might change my position...as a favor to my lover.'"

I breathed through the range of emotions this goddess's response caused. This was about saving as many lives as possible, not my old insecurities bubbling up.

Hermes clenched his jaw so tight, his veins stood out. He closed his eyes and wiped a hand down his face. "Of course, she did."

The God of Death sighed. "I told her that you were betrothed to the Oracle and that you wouldn't be doing any groveling soon."

I mustered a grateful smile. We hadn't announced our engagement, so Thanatos had to have been looking out for our relationship, and perhaps Hermes' life. The latter was the more likely of the two. Good to know his grudge had limits.

"How did she respond?" Hermes asked in a voice so soft I wouldn't be able to hear him if I weren't part harpy.

Thanatos spared me a glance; apology etched into his features. The look did my heart no favors and neither did what he said next. In Melinoë's voice, he delivered, "Since when did a marriage union stop an Olympian from seeking what they want?" Cold yet beautiful laughter followed the question. "He will come to me as I've asked, or his little bride will come to me."

Hermes buried his face in his hands.

The God of Death shivered. Using his own raspy voice, he added, "Then I got the heck out of there. Not going to lie, Melinoë scares the crap out of me."

She scared me, too. I had enough at stake without this added layer.

He then rose and took on his robed form, producing his scythe. "Welp, message delivered. I've got places to go and souls to reap."

I held out my hand. "Wait! Why did Melinoë choose you to deliver this message?" There had to be a ton of harpies and others in Hades who could do it.

The robed Thanatos shrugged. "Don't know. My best guess is that Melinoē is under the distinct impression that I have a grudge against Hermes and believed that I would deliver the message in the most annoying way possible."

Hermes lifted his head. "You still have a grudge against me?"

Thanatos's head, once again masked in shadows, shook the hood of his robe slowly. "Nah. I showed up in your bedroom just to mess with you in a fun way. If I still had a grudge, I'd have showed up earlier." With that he disappeared.

"There went that plan," Hermes sighed.

I cocked my head. "How so?"

He blinked and touched his chest, incredulity limning his handsome features. "You can't mean for me to go to her?"

The very idea of him going to someone who so willfully played with all our lives was definitely out of the question. Waving my hand in dismissal, I assured him, "No, no. Of course not."

His shoulders heaved with his sigh of relief. Rallying, Hermes rubbed his hands together. "Okay. What's the new plan?"

"I'll go the Underworld and ask her."

The dark slashes of his eyebrows mashed together, and his jaw tightened. "No."

Hermes had put all the authority a god could into that one word. Too bad I was in the habit of defying gods. Also, if we were going to be eternal life partners, he'd have to learn he couldn't just put his foot down and call it a day.

"I don't know if you know this about me, but you can't dictate what I will and won't do."

His nostrils flared, but that was the only sign I'd pissed him off. He leaned back in his chair and crossed his ankle over his knee. "I wouldn't dream of trying, but this is one thing I must beg you to please heed my advice about. No good will come of you going to Melinoë. She is feared and disliked for a reason."

"You may know her and her reputation, but I know people. She knows your character and that you would turn down cheating on me, right?"

He eyed me warily, not replying right away. Finally, the crossroads god and my love muffin relented with a cautious, "Yes."

"Her pride is bruised, but she's curious. There are questions playing in her mind: Who is this person that got you to contact her after all this time? What will you or I be willing to do for her help? Most of all, Melinoë gave the option of me asking because she wants to check me out and make me squirm a bit. I've faced enough to know I can hold my own, even among the powerful. Besides, I'll take Athena with me."

Hermes rubbed his temples. After blowing out an exasperated breath. "You'll need a guide but don't take my sister. They'll only quarrel."

I grinned. "I'm betting on it."

TWELVE

In full battle gear, Athena and Cerberus stood at either side of me at the mouth of the Kokytos. I wore similar armor to Athena, and the Nemean Lion's pelt adjusted for my harpy wings. Hermes had told us Melinoë would take the way we were dressed as a threat and that Cerberus should be enough of a deterrent. I loved the god and appreciated his advice. However, Athena and I agreed we weren't facing a goddess of nightmares and madness without protection.

While the other parts of the Underworld appeared as an eternal moonlit garden, we found ourselves in a greyscale lovechild of Salvador Dali and Tim Burton. Churning smoke-colored phantasms obscured the glittering firmament. The river, a murky shade of near black with silvery foam, carried shades that appeared as flickering images into the gaping maw of a cave. Screams and wails from the shades and phantasms echoed in my ears. Whispered nonsense and horrific suggestions trickled into my head like intrusive thoughts, causing icy pricks of fear to clamber up my spine. Every hair on my arms stood on end. The silence of the Vault got to me, but it had taken time.

"I forgot how awful this place is." Athena produced a little pouch from her armor. From within the pouch, she pulled four silken pillows of cotton the size of the end of my pinky. "Put these in your ears. You'll still be able to hear the living."

The cotton went in easy, melding into my ear canal as if liquid. All the awful sounds ceased. Athena also applied hers, and then shouted, "Do you hear me?"

Cerberus whined and nudged a head against me. *Yeah. I had no idea why she was shouting either, buddy.* I put a finger to my lips "Yes. You can talk at a normal volume."

Athena cocked her head, her delicate brow furrowing. She appeared to be confused but calm, however, her voice again came out in a shout. "I am. Why are you yelling?"

Something wasn't right. I tapped my ear. "Where did you get these?"

"Thanatos. I don't see what that has do with—" Her jaw dropped and then clamped shut, indignation hardening her features to sharp, sculpted lines. The goddess nodded curtly, indicating that she understood.

We were facing my fiancé's murderous ex, and the God of Death had jokes. Maybe after I'd lived a few thousand years, I'd get why he behaved this way. As for now, we had to press on and find Melinoë.

She whisper-shouted, "Stick close to me and keep silent for now. Because this area of the Underworld changes, I will need to steady my gaze on where we need to go and signal where we should head. You watch our surroundings."

Wasting no time, Athena lead us down the bank of the Kokytos. We walked at a brisk pace that was a hair shy of a jog. Back when I was a sedentary fortune teller, I wouldn't have been able to keep up for long, but a boost of magic and hours of daily training drills at Nicky's gymnasium made the rapid trek over unfamiliar terrain manageable.

My heart thudding in my ears, I kept up the duty of lookout, scanning the water and the skies and occasionally scoping out the surrounding landscape. There didn't seem to be anything except bizarre shapes upon the horizon. My attention stayed focused on those shapes, expecting movement or some sort of monstrosity to reveal itself. However, if I didn't look at the river or up to the roiling mass of phantasm above, the place seemed devoid of anything else remotely animated.

Suddenly, Athena stopped holding out a hand to bar my way. Not needing the goddess's warning, one of Cerberus's heads growled a low threat. The other head barked and slobbered excitedly. Meanwhile, the third head, the one closest to me, panted happily, unaware of why the other two were in a tizzy. At first, I was as clueless as the third head. Then something appeared out of the darkness of the cave.

The figure was too bulky to be humanoid in shape, at least not a bipedal one. Shadows hid the slow approaching entity, but I could somewhat make out the four legs and wings. A shudder ran through me. I'd fought a manticore and almost lost Miriam's daughter Jada in the process. Upon closer inspection, the head wasn't shaped right to be a griffin or a manticore.

Athena readied herself in a battle stance, signaling I should do the same. I unsheathed Harpe.

Cerberus leapt forward, putting himself bodily between us and the creature. He grew in size.

"Oh brother, I should've figured you'd come with her. You betrayed our parents long ago," a feminine voice scream-yowled in Greek.

If I made it out of here, I would find a way to murder the God of Death. Perhaps at least strangle him a bit, but he was going to get payback.

"And now, you dare stand between me and our mother's murderer even as she wears our brother's pelt?"

My heart lurched in my chest. I'd had the underworld dog by my side for a few years now and I forgot. I completely, utterly forgot that Echidna and Typhon were Cerberus's parents. That meant the creature on the other side of him wasn't Melinoë, but someone just as dangerous: The Sphinx.

"We seek Melinoë and have no quarrel with you," Athena shouted, also in Greek. "Fighting us goes against your sacred duties to Hades."

Bitter laughter sprang from the other side of Cerberus. "Sacred duties? You mean my eternal bondage to this place as a penance for the sins of my parents? Perhaps if I were born a simple hound and not a Sphinx with the mind of her own, I'd call it sacred duty."

My stomach knotted at the thought she was imprisoned here, forced into servitude as a guardian because of the last Titanomachy. Asking riddles and killing for King Aidoneus. The sounds of this place would drive anyone mad. My own mind swam in a sea of self-loathing for the things I'd done. In her eyes, I'd performed atrocious acts against people who'd meant me no harm. Not to mention, I'd done it all as a willing servant of her captors.

I cleared my throat. "I am sorry about your mother. Her death was an accident. She was protecting me and received a cut from Harpe in the chaos. As far as this pelt goes, I wasn't the one to kill the Nemean lion, but wearing it isn't right." As an act of good faith, I removed the pelt and held it reverently in my arms. "Cerberus, please move out of the way to let your sister take back your brother's remains."

Athena scowled in my direction but made no remark.

The Underworld hound wavered a few moments, and then finally relented, stepping aside for the Sphinx. In a greyscale realm, her fur's golden hue and her beautiful, human face shone like a sun.

I bowed my head, holding the pelt before me like an offering. Given the sphinx's reputation for violence, it was likely foolish. However, harpies and sirens had bad reps that weren't true either. This was a person whose spirit was grievously wounded. I knew that feeling. I had once walked around with a gaping hole in my chest. Hermes, Cerberus, Arachne, Nicky, Athena and so many others changed that by proving they would not also be the cause of hurt in my life. The stakes were too high to die in a fight against a sphinx. I had to be that person to her now or everyone would pay.

"I apologize for the injury I've caused and that my ancestors caused to you and your family. Echidna and Typhon never did me any harm and told me I was the key to freeing you all. I believe it wasn't just about opening Tartarus, but to free you all from all the bargains made so long ago. I promise if you spare me, I will endeavor to do that. Please, take your brother's remains as a token of my good faith." Magic prickled my skin as the oath settled in as a binding contract.

Likely feeling the magic herself, the sphinx gasped. Step by cautious step, she stalked toward me, swiping the pelt out of my hands and then backing up far enough she was out of the reach of Athena and me.

My gut turned at the notion she'd be afraid of me. It made no sense. She'd been willing to fight me moments ago. Hadn't she? I thought of the times that I'd fought despite my fears and what I'd do to protect or avenge my son, Nicky, Hermes, and even Arachne and Athena. Anyone with a heart would risk their lives for those they loved. Kill, die, do things they'd never thought they'd do.

Here was one more victim made monster over time.

"I will hold you to your promise," she said, and then disappeared into the greyscale night.

Someone slow clapped from the mouth of the cave.

Athena positioned herself in a battle stance, her spear at the ready. "Show yourself."

"Still a bossy little daddy's girl, I see," a sultry voice made of the shadow and light filtered in the earplugs. Magic laced every word and some of the dissonance the phantasms and shades caused slipped past Thanatos's defense.

I girded my mind the way that the fae prince Phyr had taught me. I imagined impenetrable layers of titanium wrapping around my head. My thoughts and feelings locked deep inside a hidden vault. I didn't unsheathe Harpe, but I kept my hand on the sword's hilt.

Laughter peeled from the darkness, echoing eerily. "Ooh, the baby has talons."

Fear slithered through me, but it was my own body's reaction, not an outside influence. Remembering I've been afraid before and still come out victorious, I lifted my chin, gaze on the darkness. "You've asked me to come, Melinoë."

Silver mist infused with smokey shadows billowed from the cave in a churning mass. Cerberus backed up, growling. Athena's gaze darted to me. She shouted something but the mist and shadows swallowed us both before the words could find me. The vapors and shadows slipped away, coalescing in to a tall, willowy woman. Half of her, including her gown, glittered silver, the other half shimmered onyx. Her eyes glowed white and onyx. Slowly, I realized that she didn't appear before me but rather, I was transported to a throne room that appeared to be a twisted nightmare replica of the Twelve's throne room in Olympus.

I swallowed hard, realizing Athena and Cerberus had not come along for the ride. This may be Persephone and Aidoneus's realm, but where we stood was Melinoë's domain. Which meant, much like Miriam had ultimate control in her faerie, this goddess had the upper hand here. Except, this wasn't the first time I'd been dragged by a supernatural to another realm to demonstrate they had more power than I had. The whole intimidation by abduction was getting real old.

Annoyed, I shoved down my fear and glanced around. "I usually don't like reproductions, but you, you really made Zeus's party room your own."

Emotion flickered in Melinoë's mismatched eyes. Rage? Surprise? Whatever sentiment filled the spark I'd witnessed, she snuffed it out with glacial indifference. She examined nails as long as talons on her silver hand. In a bored tone that would do any cartoon villain proud, she warned, "Temper your mouth, Oracle. You live at my discretion."

"I've heard that one, too." I shrugged. The warning given with no feeling was a good tactic to show how little she valued my life; however, I was absolutely finished with gods intimidating me.

Melinoë slinked her way off the dais to face me. The goddess moved with grace and preternatural stealth. One could be mesmerized by her beauty, but I faced enough predators to know one.

I blinked, and she was before me. Again, something I'd seen many supernatural do already. Standing at the same height as Hermes, the goddess forced me to look up to meet her cool gaze. At the edge of my mental defenses icy fingers glided, seeking. The goddess didn't probe further than the edge nor attempted to breach my guard, but she sure as heck wanted me to know if there was a crack, she'd slip right in.

My treacherous heart hammered in my chest. I poured more of my internal light into the mental shields. Not all of it. I wasn't dumb enough to show my entire magical hand, but I also wasn't going to allow her to sneak in the back door unaware.

Melinoë hummed and backed away, eyeing me with...was that respect? "I see Hermes is not smitten with a young fool. At least not a fool. You are young, nothing but a breath in a lifetime long as ours."

"I came here to ask if you'd help us."

"I know." She flashed her teeth. "I will not."

Impotent rage burned inside me. The trip here had been a waste of precious time.

Then something caught my eye. I stepped onto the dais and approached a window. The scene was so unlike the mad dreamscape, the throne room, and other parts of Hades, I could hardly believe what I saw.

The shades that seemed tortured and broken on the other side drifted off the river onto banks where the wraiths greeted them. They had a look of utter peace as they walked off into a beautiful garden beyond the shores.

"The disquiet of their mind no longer plagues them here."

I turned to Melinoë. "You heal them?"

She nodded. "It comes with a price."

"The realm before the cave?"

"My peace," she whispered. "Their nightmares become mine. Their delusions haunt me. I fixed your mother's shade. Did Persephone tell you that?"

"Thank you." I took her glimmering obsidian hand and squeezed. Her skin felt as soft and real as any other hand I held. Yet the power of a god pulsed from her.

At first, she seemed shocked and then just held my hand. It was bizarre but felt like the right thing to do.

"Why do you do it?"

She tilted her head and her mismatched gaze met mine. "You plan on sacrificing yourself for the mortal world and you ask this of me?"

It was a silly question. "Because those in a position of power of leadership are servants. The good ones, at least."

She nodded.

"Apollo will ruin the lives of everyone, kill the Fates themselves, to achieve ascension. He must be stopped."

"Then win. No one will have faith in the sun if it does not shine." Her cold fingers squeezed. At first, it was gentle but suddenly her grip grew uncomfortably tight. Something flashed in her eyes and her eyes turned feral. A wild peal of laughter escaped her lips. "Then again, if I win, I could be the sun and moon. Hermes would be mine again, and you would be dust."

The tentative tendrils that had poked at my defenses now slammed harder than Scylla smashed Atlantis. I shielded, left hand unsheathing Harpe. "Let go."

Melinoë's head thrashed back and forth. Her face flickered and changed into other faces.

My heart raced. I didn't know what to do. Killing her for something that seemed out of her control was not the answer, but I had no recourse. She had me in her grip.

"Melinoë!" I shouted. "We are not enemies. I came here for your help, not to fight."

She let go of my hand. Breathing hard and pressing her temples, she took several steps back, her gaze shifting wildly about like an animal suddenly caught in a trap, but she was fully herself in appearance. "You must go...Now!"

I looked to the left and right, not seeing an exit.

A wraith appeared seemingly out of nowhere. "Come."

I didn't question the figure or that I needed to get out of there.

Following them through a part in the shadows, I found Cerberus and Athena waiting on the other side. Thanatos was with them. He nodded at the wraith and flipped a coin to the dark figure. A skeletal hand snatched the coin, before the wraith disappeared altogether.

"Will she help?" Athena asked after giving me a once over.

I shook my head.

"You're alive, which means you got her good side. Time to go home before her other aspect shows up," Thanatos said, cutting open a portal to my house with his scythe.

"Oh, I met the other." I shuddered, rushing through the opening between planes of reality. Cerberus galloped at my side.

"No. You didn't," Athena, not far behind, assured. "You're still alive and seem mentally intact."

"Thanks for the vote of confidence."

CHAPTER

THIRTEEN

I held the javelin over my shoulder, trying not to think about the mental duress Melinoë had to endure. Hermes explained that the goddess absorbed what plagued every beleaguered shade that entered her realm so that the shade, in death, could know peace. Unfortunately, it did something to her, splitting her between the goddess she'd been born as and an entity that manifested. That entity is what Thanatos had spoken to. I believed despite what she might turn into sometimes that she was the underworld guardian of the deeply disturbed. Maybe she'd said no but would be an ally later. As long as she didn't manifest as that other being... whatever it was had the gods scared. I was afraid, too.

Would challenging him be enough? The Fates seemed to think so. Would winning be enough? Melinoë was sure of it. All I could do was focus on now, improving at one of my three chosen areas of competition.

I inhaled. On the exhale, I heaved the spear. The javelin launched, taking flight, throttling into the air, hitting the arc point and the descent. I held my breath. The javelin did not land next to Athena's mark...but a good distance past hers! An eruption of butterflies burst from my stomach into my chest, escaping my lips in a screech of victory.

Athena clapped me on the back, as she let out her own jubilant cry. All harpy eyes, and soon others, landed on me. They gathered around congratulating me. The joy on their faces for this small win infected my erstwhile troubled mind with newfound hope.

However, a loud whine cut the moment short. Silence blanketed over the gymnasium. Throttling through the air at an incredible speed a glowing object zipped above our heads, slowing until it hovered ominously over my javelin. It was Athena's owl. *Apollo's* response.

Hermes appeared at my side, sliding an arm around my shoulders. He squeezed gently. I slid an arm around his waist, leaning my head against him. Arachne skittered next to Athena, who hadn't left my other side. Nora found a place between them. Nicky settled herself between Athena and I, giving me a reassuring nod. I didn't miss the quiver in her lip.

"Spot," Arachne called. "Get up!"

Cerberus, who'd been napping, shook his heads. He took note of the owl and trotted over, plopping his backside on my feet and pushing the head closest to me against my hand. Another of his heads whined, while the third growled softly in the direction of the owl.

Although my heart raced from the anticipation, I couldn't help but feel comforted by the overwhelming number of supportive presences in my life.

The owl projected Kronos on Zeus's throne with Apollo to the right and Dione seated where Cronos had sat. Apollo stared straight ahead but I could see he wasn't happy. I exchanged glances with Hermes and Athena.

"Do they play musical chairs on Olympus now?" Arachne muttered.

Several within earshot chuckled nervously. My own laughter

died in my throat, choked by the fear of what this new development might mean.

Traces of what had grown oh so familiar to me in my beloved Hermes's features were set in the lines of a face that wasn't as cold as the last message but wasn't friendly either. A being Hermes could call grandfather, yet he wasn't like the other gods I'd come to know at all. Universes swirled in the depths of Cronos's eyes. As he seemed to stare directly at me, my mind struggled to not to drown in the infinite that existed there. Apollo, I could take. I was confident of that. But, it had taken all of the Twelve Olympians working in harmony to defeat this primordial being in the Titanomachy.

My erstwhile victory, the javelin toss that had given me so much hope, paled in the presence of such might. We were well and royally screwed.

After a few more moments of intense staring, Cronos nodded to Dione. The Titan grinned at him. My grandmother turned that pleasant smile to me.

"We agreed to your terms, Lydia."

Nothing had changed. My freedom, Luke's freedom was still at stake. Why was she smiling? She'd be imprisoned in that realm where the fates lived. Who could smile at an eternity weaving, measuring, and cutting? Is this what she wanted all along? To have her children freed only to imprison herself with her recent descendants? It made no sense.

Apollo cleared his throat.

Dione cut the god a sharp look but said nothing. Cronos shifted his massive body in his seat and nodded again at her. She gave him a look I couldn't quite read.

"One additional term—every member of the former Twelve, even those who have abdicated, must compete."

～

A RANCH-STYLE, wooden sign hung over a dirt road just past the town of Sequim. In bold letters, it read Demeter's Lavender Farm and it was held up by a likeness of the goddess on one side and Zeus on the other. The farm was close enough to Milagro Bay that I decided to drive rather than pop in and out of the space-time continuum or let Athena send an owl...or do something wild like call. Hermes sat in the passenger seat, resting his elbow on the door and propping his chin on his fist pensively. Cerberus and Athena sat in the back. The latter of the two silent. Cerberus licked the window with the single head of his black Labrador guise. Nicky was going to make me wash that. It felt good to get away from training, the temple, and just everything in general. Driving cleared my head and reminded me how I got caught up in all of this in the first place.

"Kinda on the nose with the name, isn't it?" I remarked.

Hermes shrugged one shoulder.

"It *is* Demeter's lavender farm," Athena said, speaking for the first time since we got in the car. "Why would the goddess of the harvest name it anything else? —oh! There's Hestia! Sound the warning signal."

I did as she bid, honking at Hestia. The goddess looked up from attending her beehives at the border of the property and waved. Hestia had made a lucrative business of selling lavender honey and handmade soaps online. She didn't live here, so we'd planned on hitting up her house down the road next.

"At least we get to kill two birds with one stone."

Athena in the rearview and Hermes in my peripheral assumed shocked expressions. I rolled my eyes.

"It's an expression. It means that we'll get two jobs done at once."

We pulled up to the main building, a big farmhouse, within a complex of processing and equipment buildings, and green houses. The house was painted with navy blue shutters. Each window had a box filled with flowers. Steps led to a wraparound porch. There, Zeus sat in a rocking chair, reading.

We didn't have to say a word.

The former king of the gods snapped his book shut and ran a hand through his gray curls. The book disappeared as he rose. His faded overalls and flannel shirt also vanished, replaced by his chiton and a golden laurel crown. "If they won't allow me to abdicate, there is no sense in pretense."

Demeter appeared from a shed, also dressed as an Olympian. Her matronly face was as resolved as that of the former king. However, when Hestia arrived, she was still in her white beekeeper coveralls, her eyes luminous. She took all of us in, spreading her gloved hands. "Surely I can't be called to the games?"

I gave her rueful smile. "All of the Twelve, I'm afraid."

The goddess gave her beehives in the distance a mournful glance. Expression far less resolute than the others, she donned her clothes from Olympus. "I was quite content with my life here."

Demeter nodded in agreement. "The novelty would have taken at least a few centuries to wear off."

FOURTEEN

My stomach twisted in knots as I watched my Luke getting into a black SUV. The vehicle was one of ten carrying supes from Earth that would set up the games, and I.S.E.A agents who would set up the camera systems through the portal to The Vault. The stakes hadn't changed but the upcoming games became more real as I watched the vehicles disappear from this world, departing to the place where he and I spent months imprisoned and isolated. Tears slid down my cheeks. There had to be a way out of serving as the Fates. Luke and I, even Dione, deserved better than an eternal imprisonment.

Juan leaned in, wrapping an arm around my shoulders and gifting me with a generous side hug. "We have to trust this is for the best, mamita."

"Aren't I supposed to be encouraging you? It's your husband going in..." My mouth suddenly dry, I swallowed hard and then nodded to the last vehicle crossing over. "There."

His warm smile soothed like a balm to my worried mother's heart. "You always encourage us. Besides, we're grown. I can return the favor."

THE SUPERNATURAL COUNCIL of the Americas held a press conference about the games in a downtown Seattle hotel banquet room. We sat at a table in the front of the room, facing a sea of press agents both seated and standing in the back. I.S.E.A agents spread throughout the room, serving as security on multiple levels. Jada and Roxy were junior agents now and among them. Shawn, Phyr, and Micah stood behind us as the council's personal guard. It was all overkill. Everyone who sat at this table could wipe out the humans before us.

That was a scary thought.

I made an initial statement, declaring the games and the intent. Of course, I left out the consequences and the potential threat the world was under. To the public, this was a sporting event. Then we started fielding questions.

"If these games are in another universe, how will they be relayed to Earth?"

"We have a magical-tech team working on that," Gabriel replied.

Some of the press looked bemused. Others had follow-up questions.

Miriam leaned toward her mic. "The science involved is beyond what is so far known by mundanes on Earth. To understand is difficult even for those who are adept in the field, but I'll try to break it down..."

Without any shame, I zoned out. I didn't care how humans were going to see us fight for our lives. I didn't care much about these press conferences either. This was only to fulfill the promise to the supes. Part of me hoped Luke would rig it so they saw none of the games on this side. We were participating to save everyone's lives, not gain more power through mundane admiration. I could barely manage mine.

Princess nudged my arm. She put a hand over her mic and whispered. "They asked about Carlo and the Renee Charles murder."

Shawn, the council's enforcer and lawyer, stepped between us and stole my mic. "No comment. Next question."

After the press conference, we appeared on the talk show circuit, the Jenna Jones Show, and numerous other internet and television news networks. I had a myriad of solo interviews as well.

To my chagrin, my former life as Carlo's wife and the murder of Renee Charles came up. Every. Single. Time.

Shawn coached me on how to answer the questions. I taught him a thing or two in evasive speech. Soon the two of us were coaching the council on how to field questions. Miriam had a thing about truth. Her fae blood wouldn't allow her to lie and her morals made it a bit hard for us to find work arounds, but she got the hang of using her words carefully. Honest but cautious was our policy.

Rhiannon the rock witch was *not* allowed to speak to the media.

While we played supernatural celebrities, Phyr, Jada, Hecate, witches, and I.S.E.A mages on this side worked with Luke and his team to find a way to broadcast the games to Earth.

Whenever we weren't hyping the games to global audiences, we were training. We endured months of this, waiting for the builders to return.

Every night, I fell asleep as soon as my head hit the pillow. Well, not every night. Some nights I spent making passionate or gentle love with Hermes. During the quiet minutes after we were satiated and basking in the afterglow, intrusive thoughts of losing him in the games slipped in. I had nightmares where he died by his brother's or sometimes his grandfather's hands, but I refused to believe these bad dreams were portents from my Oracular gift. We would part only if I didn't find a way to avoid The Fates.

After a particularly gruesome nightmare depicting Hermes's demise, I woke with a start. Hermes, alive and well, shifted in his sleep but didn't wake. I tried to sleep, but my mind wouldn't settle after what it made up. Careful not to disturb him, I removed the covers and plodded downstairs to the kitchen.

Cerberus, cured up in his dog bed, snored. Arachne sat at the table, knitting. She didn't sleep much. Some ancient beings didn't sleep at all. I grinned at the normalcy of the scene—well, normal to me. Most people do not have a spider lady and three-headed monster pooch in their house.

"The water in the kettle should be hot enough for tea."

I collected a favorite mug, a pale pink one with a starfish relief. Hermes had picked the mug for me in a souvenir shop in Cannon Beach, Oregon. That weekend getaway with just the two of us and Cerberus seemed so long ago. A warm bubble of happiness filled my chest at the memory of Cerberus and Hermes running the beach and over the turbulent water to Haystack Rock and back to me. Neither the dog nor the god got any of my Goonies references, so I had to show them the movie and take them to Astoria so they could see "the house."

After pouring myself a mug with a heavy dose of honey to sweeten the tea, I sat at the table with Arachne in companionable silence.

The steady click of her needles stopped. She looked at me over the frame of her thick glasses. "Something ain't right if you're sitting here me with me instead of in bed with the hunk. Might as well spill it."

My gaze fell to my mug. "I keep dreaming that Hermes dies in the games."

Arachne resumed her knitting. "Same dream or different?"

"Different."

"So, you're wondering if it's the unconscious tapping into the threads of the Fates' weave or is it just anxiety?"

Biting my lip, I shrugged and then lifted my teacup. My hand shook, spilling some of the hot liquid on the table. Arachne put her knitting aside and grabbed a towel, mopping up the mess before I could do it.

"I think. I don't know what to think." I set the mug down on the clean surface and rested my face on my palms.

"Well then, the more important question is, can you prevent it from happening?"

"No. I'm not able to prevent it from happening." My eyes stung and my body shook until I released the tears. Losing Hermes was always a possibility, but the surety of it in my dreams...

A gentle hand stroked my back. Once I got my emotions out, Arachne handed me a hand-woven tissue. I'd learned I couldn't say no to these because she had a million of them. Literally. Instead of protesting, I dried my eyes and blew my nose. Meanwhile, Arachne resumed her chair and her knitting. "I'm going to say something you won't want to hear, but I'm going to say it for your own good."

I spread my hands, welcoming her to speak her mind.

"There is no such thing as a hero. They're written as such after the fact. All you can do is your best and accept that none of this is truly in your hands."

I nodded.

"And another thing," she looked at me above her thick framed glasses. "The Moirai have their own agenda. They know Apollo wants to replace them. He hasn't been subtle."

My stomach knotted. I hadn't even considered the Fates might want to sway me for their own reasons. The knot set on fire, burning with rage. "I'm getting really sick of these over-powered gods thinking they can use me as their pawn in their games."

"Careful now," Arachne said without pausing her knitting. "Don't melt your wings there, Icarus. In all of this, don't do the right thing. Do the thing that is right for who you love and who you want to see make it through."

FIFTEEN

Arachne sped through the gymnasium, past Zeus and Hermes sparring, past the harpies drilling, past Cerberus napping on a mat, and past Hestia and Demeter practicing leap dances. I watched her eight spider feet scurrying toward me as I collapsed after the gazillionth pushup Athena made Nora and I do.

"The Vault is ready!"

Every head within earshot turned to look at the spider-human in the florescent pink muumuu and neon blue curlers bouncing in her white hair. No one asked who was back. We all knew. Butterflies dancing in my stomach, I pushed to my feet.

Everyone who had a phone pulled out theirs or ran to retrieve them. I watched a video of Luke being interviewed from a reporter on Earth. There, my star boy fielded her questions with ease. It seemed as if he were right here. The magical tech worked. The world would see us compete...possibly die.

I scrolled through articles.

Power, rule, *everything* was up for grabs. However, they were still treating this as if it were only a sporting event. The only sporting event that predicted more views than any game in the history of the world.

My gaze swung to Hermes. The games still felt like something far off, a distant challenge. Now we were going to face Apollo, the Titans, and all the other supes. I wasn't foolish enough to believe the new rulers of Olympus were the only ones to fear. A niggling voice whispered, *"Is your best enough to keep him alive?"*

An invisible cord looped around my throat, cutting off my air. I took the cord and wrapped it around the small voice, strangling it. I had no time for self-doubt.

From there everything was a blur of activity. While we packed to leave for the Vault, notifications lit up my phone. Some were coordination efforts. Some were news alerts I'd signed up to receive. Every sort of social media and news outlet around the globe buzzed with news of the games.

Soon we were loaded up in SUVs, and in what seemed like a blink I was there, back in the Vault. The magic of the place a palpable, ever-present thing. We unloaded and got into lines. Supes from across the multiverse gathered in lines, led by I.S.E.A agents to dorms.

I shuddered internally, hoping that they made the 'dorms' better than the cell I'd spent months in.

Agents weren't just leading teams. I.S.E.A had reps everywhere. They were a supposedly a neutral, mundane security. I wondered what they could do against supernaturals, but the thought was squashed by the realization this had been their facility. Only the angels surpassed their knowledge of how to run it. Perhaps it was a good thing Melinoë refused to set a trap. The agents might discover a trap before we could put it to use and have a pseudo-ally turned out.

The agent in charge of our group led us through a door into a hall. Since all of the agents used the same door and our group were the only ones on the other side, the door must have been a portal to a different part of the Vault. My mind took a second to process that thought. Any door in here could lead anywhere else within the facility.

"How did the door take us here?" Nora asked, voicing my thoughts.

The agent, a young blonde woman with a pleasant face, flashed a thousand-watt smile. She spoke with a thick Texan accent when she said, "To tell you the truth, I don't know, hun." She tapped her forehead. "I picture where I want to go, and the door always opens where I need it to."

Hermes and I exchanged a glance. Athena arched an eyebrow. Her down-home, wholesome act might work on mundanes, but this was bullshit, and we knew it. She did a great job of ushering all to our rooms. There was no sense in pushing the issue with her. Security couldn't play favorites. We were all the away team here.

"Your names are on the doors to your quarters. Before you enter, touch the door and think about the most relaxing environment you've been in. Give the room a sec to get ready. The door will notify you when it's done prepping the perfect domicile while you stay here."

A small sigh of relief escaped my lips. Not a soulless blank cell with a bed and toilet. We all dispersed. Within a few moments, everyone found their doors. Disappearing into hers, Nora exclaimed, "Hot damn. I could get used to this."

Hermes grinned and a spark twinkled in his eyes as he reached for the door marked 'Lydia and Hermes.' "May I?"

I spread my hands and couldn't help but grin back at him. "Be my guest."

It wasn't like the cell or anything like home. The room reminded me a lot of Hermes's chambers in the palace on Olympus, lush bedding, plush chairs, soft music, and the sound of rushing water in the background. On closer inspection, an adjacent bathroom housed a waterfall pouring into a massive tub. The space was peaceful. A place where we could rest. Yet, I walked around with my bag, taking it in but not settling into any space.

Hermes followed me, taking my bag from my shoulder. He set it inside an armoire next to his. The clothes and belongings started hanging themselves.

I watched as I paced the room.

The god blocked my path and settled his hands on my shoulders. "Let's talk about what's keeping you up at night. Discussing it might help."

My breath caught in my throat. I thought I'd been hiding my worry from him. A grimace tugged at the corners of my mouth. "I've had bad dreams."

He hooked a finger under my chin and lifted it so I'd meet his dark-eyed gaze. "Is it me or Luke who dies in these dreams?"

I swallowed down the lump in my throat. Still my voice broke on the one word. "You."

He placed a gentle kiss on my forehead and swiped a tear from my cheek. "Please don't hide things from me. Not all dreams of an Oracle are prophetic and if they are, we will face and divert the path together."

Nodding, I grinned. "You're right. I should've told you."

"You spent many years bearing all the responsibility, making yourself useful rather than asking for the same out of your partner. You don't have to do that now. Not for me or for anyone. I have your back and front, so do our friends."

I knew it, but it was good to hear—especially now that I had more than Luke's doctor's appointments, homework, or sleep schedule to worry about. I cupped the god's cheek. "We will live through this, and I will marry you, Hermes, son of Zeus, I swear."

The magic of my promise settled into my flesh and bone, becoming part of me. The binding magic also affected him. For what seemed like an eternity, he stared at me mouth agape that I'd made such oath. In a blur of movement, one second I was on the floor facing the god that I loved. The next, I was on the bed lying beneath his large body, his lips hovering over mine.

CHAPTER
SIXTEEN

Playtime and rest didn't last long. We woke in a tangle to a hologram standing at the foot of the bed—a human woman in a white gown, brown hair, and smiling face. Her features were uncannily similar to traits that ran in my family. I was certain it was no coincidence.

"Hello contestants Lydia, Oracle to the Gods, and Hermes, Son of Zeus, God of the Crossroads, tricksters, thieves and former Psychopomp. You will be interviewed by the Supernatural Games officiants in thirty minutes and in forty minutes, individually and respectively." The hologram flashed an eerie imitation of a smile. "The entire world and beyond will be watching. Please dress appropriately."

The hologram then flickered out.

Hermes and I gave each other a glance before disentangling and readying in a hurry. I was too nervous to do much talking, and my lover, poetic as he could be, didn't like to speak when he was in the middle of a task.

My name appeared on the door. I peered over my shoulder at Hermes. "I guess I'll see you in a half hour?"

The God of the Crossroads had narrowed his eyes at the door, suspicion evident. Upon shifting his gaze to meet mine, he managed a reassuring smile that didn't reach his eyes. "You'll do fine."

I gave him a peck on the cheek. "So will you."

The door opened the moment I stepped in front of it. Ready, I stepped through.

On the other side, I found myself in what looked like a television studio. A team of humans worked cameras and lights, all focused on a dais. Contestants from different worlds sat on the bleachers upon the dais: an angel dressed uncannily like a Power Ranger, a fae in what looked like fencing gear, a Norse goddess by her armor and furs, and some beings I didn't recognize were already seated. No one from team Earth appeared to be present. My pulse quickened at the sight of Melinoë and Apollo among the crowd. In front of the bleachers, Jenna Jones wore a sharp business suit, and her hair was cut in stylish layers. The talk show host sat in an armchair opposite another empty armchair, and a small coffee table rested between.

For a moment, I didn't feel like I was in the Vault, but the moment didn't last. Even though this place was no longer a prison, the magic imbued in the very fabric of pressed upon me much in the same way one could walk underwater but you never forgot it could drown you.

Jenna flashed a brilliant set of perfect teeth in my direction and stood. "Ah, the founder of the games is here!" She clapped. Holographic words flashed behind me, cueing those assembled on the bleachers to stand and applaud. The contestants scowled and frowned. The lights flashed again and again.

"We're live streaming. Goodwill in games is important to humans." A male voice came out of the dark behind the cameras. The voice echoed in several languages.

The other supernaturals rose and applauded. Apollo smiled at me. Melinoë stood but her gaze was on the space where I'd entered. *Did she see Hermes in our room? Would that hurt or help us?* Pushing those thoughts aside and raising my mental shields, I approached the dais on shaky legs. Jenna embraced me as if we were longtime friends. In my ear, the host whispered, "Don't worry about stage directions. All extraneous noise will be filtered out and though it's live, there's lag so we edit real time. They'll look like they applauded you immediately. Now smile. You look like a cow corralled in the slaughterhouse."

With a deep breath, I put on my Oracle face—a Mona Lisa-esque grin accompanied by an air of the otherworldly in my eyes. At least that's what I tried to project. I probably looked like a grinning, cross-eyed fool as I took the chair opposite of Jenna Jones. She adjusted her pantsuit as she returned to her seat.

"What inspired you to form these games?"

"The world knows we have power and skills that are extraordinary, but they haven't seen us use them. Games have always been the way of the people I descend from. Competition takes us from merely beings who use our skills for survival and turns them into a form of art to master. The arts separate us from baser creatures and shows we have higher thinking. Supernaturals are like humans in this way. Through these games, we can show that we are different yet the same, striving for excellence in practicing our innate gifts." The question wasn't new, neither was the answer. So the words came out with ease.

"Besides predicting the future, what gifts could you possibly have that would warrant your participation?"

My mouth went dry. I wasn't ever asked this before. Everyone assumed I was an Oracle and that was that. I'd never discussed being a harpy queen or that I was the granddaughter of a Titan and the daughter of an unknown line. My gift of lightning hands wasn't something I'd shared in any press interview either.

A smug smile caught my attention in the periphery. Apollo sat forward, grinning ear to ear. *Happy to hear what I had to say, Jerk face?*

I swallowed hard. What did I have to say? I could hedge and allude without giving up too much. However, this was a game of power. It wouldn't hurt that people knew what I was, what I could do. Not thinking I was a shoo-in would be more of a problem than giving up too much before the actual competition. Underdogs couldn't win if the belief odds were stacked against them.

"I am more than an Oracle. I am also a harpy queen and a Titaness."

Jenna's eyes flared. "That's a lot more than we knew. What is a Titaness?"

"An older kind of god than the Olympians. The Titan Dione is my grandmother. I'd guess you'd call me a demigod but that denotes my magic is watered down. It's not. Most people are not one single thing, but rather an amalgamation of their ancestors' traits, skills, and culture."

The talk show host licked her lips and leaned forward. "Care to demonstrate for the world what someone of your...background can do?"

Uh oh. She'd taken the bait a little too well.

"You'd like me to demonstrate my powers before the competition?" I gestured to the bleachers and then gave her a pointed look. "Are you going to ask the same of everyone?"

Jenna crossed her legs, eyes sharpening. She'd underestimated me. "I suppose—"

"The rest of us gods and demigods are well known," Apollo interrupted, in a tone oozing with confidence. "If someone wants to know what we can do or anything about us, they can look us up on the internet. You, on the other hand, are an unknown, a wild card."

I'd love to zap the smug look right off his handsome face. He was responsible for all of this. His vainglory addled brain killed my mother, Thetis, and who knew how many others in his quest to become an ascended god.

Looking at the camera, I replied, "I am, even to the gods. I prefer to remain that way until the time comes to show you all that I can do."

"If she gives a small demonstration," Apollo countered, grinning at the rest of the contestants. "I'm sure all of us are willing to give one as well."

I held up my hands and stood. "Fine. I will demonstrate one of my gifts."

Jenna clapped her hands.

Closing my eyes, I shut out the others. I pictured my mother's broken shade, the women before me who died, I heard Luke's voice saying goodnight when we were trapped in this place, the real Renee's dead body on the news, and I envisioned what would happen to Earth if I should lose—Hermes's demise and me, Luke, and Dione trapped as the Fates came unbidden. Rage unlike that I'd ever known, unlike anything Carlo could ever induce, filled me. Apollo wanted ultimate power and didn't care who he harmed.

The odor of ozone filled my nostrils. Crackling filled my ears. I opened my eyes to lightning bolts dancing around my body in a perfect sphere. My flesh unharmed. The demonstration lasted less than a minute but was enough.

"Since when can you harness my father's gift?" The indignation in Apollo's tone resonated through the room in a loud boom.

I grinned directly at him dimming the light show as easily as someone flipped a switch. "Your father wasn't the only one with that gift. However, Zeus certainly has secretly helped me harness our shared innate ability since he took refuge on my world."

The wheels turning in Apollo's head spun so fast, I swore smoke was about to come out his ears.

That's right. Banishing daddy and the other Olympians led to me learning how to be better at a lot of things.

Taking his sweet time to declare war might have been a good strategy for the long lived. However, that same strategy didn't account for how fast someone who grew up in the mortal world learned.

CHAPTER

SEVENTEEN

After a day of interviews, the following day we got to assemble as a team in an arena. I sent out the invitation but I.S.E.A agents and the supes from the various worlds ran everything and designed the games. Looking around at the teams, the drone cameras, and agents behind the scenes running around and calling the shots, I fully comprehended how many elements were out of my control with the games, causing my stomach to knot. However, the setup was fair to those who didn't know that Apollo wanted to use the games as a means to become one of the ascended.

There were hundreds of teams in the arena, each assigned a color. The Earth supernatural team was designated the color red. We found a red circle and gathered there as the other teams found their colors. Hermes and I weren't the only ones to have red shirts and track-pants appear in our rooms in the morning.

"Oh, shit! We're the red shirts on this mission," Miriam said with a grin and a wink.

Gabriel chuckled along with some other Earth born sci-fi geeks. However, unlike everyone else the amusement didn't reach the were-nephil's eyes. Phyr laughed too, markedly late as if it took him an extra moment to get the joke.

Then he remarked for the benefit of the others who didn't laugh, "A reference to the long running space exploration program called Star Trek. It is humorous because the red shirts are the crew members slated to die on missions requiring them to leave the safety of a spaceship." His amber eyes twinkled as he turned his gaze to Miriam. "Very funny, but your joke shows your faeness. Others may be appalled by the way you suggest we are slated to die, anam cara."

"It's not funny at all if you explain it," Princess quipped, her voice a near snarl. Her gaze was on the Unseelie fae court and the shifter named Carmen with them.

"I appreciated the explanation. Quite amusing, Miriam," Athena chimed in and then laughed. It was a brief uttering of, "hahaha", and utterly stiff as the goddess herself, but genuine. Zeus didn't laugh, but he smiled at his daughter's amusement. Demeter gave the witchy fae a condescending smile. Hestia giggled. Hermes laced his fingers with mine, a small grin tugging at his own mouth. I allowed myself to laugh. If the battle goddesses Athena and the Mórrígan could be amused so could I.

Agents Tan, Doyle, and Roanhorse stepped onto a raised platform with a podium. Tan, dressed in her usual black suit spoke with her Boston accent, "Welcome to the first Supernatural Games."

Her voice filled the stadium as if amplified by a mic and sound system. A black globe, one of the camera drones, I assumed circled her head. Many more flew above the gathered supes. The magical technology of this place wasn't left unappreciated.

"We are not only live-streaming this event to Earth, but to every world represented here today."

Applause and cheers rose from the assembled supernaturals. Some stomped on the floor. Others bellowed or howled their delight. I didn't understand why they were excited. Belief from Earth was the goal, right?

"Not only will they all feel support from Earth, but where they are the leaders of their home worlds," Miriam whispered, mostly for my benefit since I was the newest supe on the block.

"Smart move on I.S.E.A's part," Athena replied. "Less focus on Earth."

"More pressure on us though," Nicky spoke up from behind me. "Everything and everyone is up for grabs now."

I hadn't even considered belief from other worlds as a factor. I'd centered humans. I'd thought that Earth was the prize. Had Apollo known it would go this way? My head spun and the floor seemed to drop from beneath me, yet I remained standing, holding hands with Hermes. As if sensing my distress, he squeezed my hand. I was grateful for the pressure, bringing me back into my body and the moment.

"The contestants in the games will compete individually in the initial rounds. Those who come in last for the initial rounds will be disqualified from competing further in the games. If everyone on your team comes in last during the initial rounds, your team will be escorted back to your home world."

I swallowed hard and exchanged a glance with Hermes.

"The final round will be a team sport. The winning team will go on to the next round and the losing team will be escorted home, until we are down to two supernatural teams. Those teams will play in a final challenge, demonstrating magical prowess, physical strength and speed, and the ability to work as a team. At the end of the games, the winning team will have multi-verse wide recognition and unlimited access to Earth."

Agent Tan struggled with the last part of the final sentence. It must have hit her the way it hit me that we might not win. What was not said was that the winning team would have unlimited access to a world obsessed with physical prowess of athletes and adding a supernatural element would raise them higher than any athlete in the history of the world. Given the physiques of the gods present, perhaps it was the same all over the multiverse. In the scope of things, Nora and I were the weakest links on our team. I had *just* gotten good at javelin. I had *just* learned to use my lightning effectively.

Agent Roanhorse said something behind Tan. The agent gestured for him to take her place. He gave the crowd a look that had a lot more menace than any human should muster in a crowd of deadly supernaturals. Then again, he was an I.S.E.A agent. He'd dealt with our kind all the time. "My colleague left out a very important rule: If a contestant willingly uses magic or any other means to murder a member of another team, then their entire team is disqualified."

"What about accidents?" asked someone among from Hell's team —an amalgamation of darkly ethereal Fallen and four appendages, ruby-skinned demons. My bet it was the Prince of Darkness himself. Miriam's eyeroll in Gabriel's direction, and some of his angels bristling in the background, confirmed it.

"Clarify your question, King Lucifer of Gehenna, Hell," Roanhorse answered, stone faced.

No crown adorned his head, but a fallen angel with inky wings and ebony mist at his feet broke from the rest of the demons and Fallen of his team. He was beautiful in a gothic sort of way but so freaking creepy, I couldn't see how Miriam ever slept with him. Then again, I'd been married to Carlo for years. I glanced at Hermes and then at Gabriel and Phyr, both of Miriam's lovers sidling closer to her. Each looked like they were willing to be disqualified. One of us had taste that had certainly changed. It was me. My god was a poetic sweetie.

Miriam still liked them pretty...and scary as heck.

Lucifer spread his hands in a graceful movement, his beatific face putting Renaissance painting to shame. "We should all expect the games to challenge our limits which means there will be a certain element of danger. Sometimes our magic acts in our defense without conscious direction. Think of it as a fight or flight response. Will there be punishment for someone dying as the result of an accidental death in these circumstances?"

Miriam cursed softly in a language I couldn't understand but could fully follow. Gabriel stiffened. Phyr gripped the air where the hilt of Angel's Bane would be.

Agent Tan stepped forward; her face dourer than I'd ever seen it. The unseen magic projected her voice as she answered in an authoritative tone, "Any deaths will disqualify the opposing team until an official, unbiased investigation is conducted and is ruled an accident."

Murmurs rang out through the crowd.

I had the sudden feeling of being watched. Turning on instinct, my gaze landed on the team from the Underworld. Melinoë stared at where my hand was linked with Hermes. Rage twisted her beautiful features.

Like a ghoul dancing on a grave, a frisson grazed my shoulders.

Persephone spoke to her. Her hand clasped the other goddess's arm in a vise grip and the queen's chest glowed as she spoke—her chest had also glowed when she controlled my mother's shade in Asphodel. King Aidoneus held up a hand. Something dark and inky slithered between him and Melinoë.

Sirens slipped silently in the way, forming a barrier which blocked me from the scene, and Melinoë's building wrath.

Around us, the teams broke up into smaller groups. The speech was over, and everyone had already started to mingle. Supes from opposing teams greeted each other like old friends. Even Miriam, Gabriel, and Phyr spoke with Lucifer.

How did I miss the end? The thought that it might have been Melinoë in my head, distracting me, made me check my mental shields.

"We should go," Hermes urged, his face grim and his eyes haunted.

"Good idea." Thanatos appeared seemingly out of nowhere. He jerked a bony thumb in the direction of the Underworld team. "It's taking both of them to control it."

"It was foolish to bring her," Athena scolded, as we made our way away from the mingling crowd toward the exit.

Thanatos spread his hands. "I've been saying this the whole time. The thing is she's a wild card, but a good one against the Titans."

Athena scoffed. "Her power won't do us any good if she murders Lydia, or anyone else for that matter."

"She's had her chaos under control for centuries," Hermes argued, glancing over his shoulder.

I looked, too. All the gods and monsters roaming about the arena gave the team from the Underworld a wide berth.

Athena obstructed my view, throwing up her hands. "Chaos can't be controlled. It's why they call it chaos."

CHAPTER

EIGHTEEN

We retreated to a multi-purpose room, dedicated to our team only. Thanatos couldn't pass through the door, and he wasn't allowed his scythe until the games, so he couldn't create a portal to join us inside. "What if I have to be in a round with her?" I asked no one in particular, pacing the perimeter of the room.

Hermes plopped on a sofa and buried his face in his hands. Nora and Athena headed to a display. Arachne skittered across the floor lowering herself into a papasan. A bag of yarn and knitting needles appeared on a table next to the chair. The elderly monster picked up her supplies and got to work. "Melinoë may be able to keep control —" She gave me a pointed look over her cat-eye framed glasses. "—if Hermes isn't there being all lovey-dovey with you."

"Perhaps, " I agreed. I passed a hand over Hermes's head as I walked by. He reached up and stroked it.

I'd argue with Arachne that holding hands wasn't an inappropriate public display of affection, but she had a point. Not long ago there was a time that I would've seen red if I saw Carlo with another woman. Perhaps in Melinoë's mind she was alright with me but

108

seeing Hermes with someone else hurt so bad that it melted the mental walls she must have to put up to stay sane after absorbing all the ills of the shades.

A lump formed in my throat. I wasn't so callous as to not feel sympathy for the goddess's struggle with jealousy and heartbreak. By the way Hermes sank in a chair and held his face between his hands, he wasn't immune to her pain either. The whole situation sucked, and this added level of tension didn't help.

Athena wandered to the kitchenette. There, she stared at some instructions and then asked a dispenser, "Four hot coffees. Two with cream and sugar. One black. One with a touch of cream, please." A cup appeared and coffee ran from a spout. She faced Arachne. "Lydia and Hermes have done nothing wrong. He ended that relationship long ago. Her rage is not about their affection for each other but that side of her used my sweet brother and now doesn't have him to quench her thirst."

Nora followed the goddess. Athena handed her the tea and asked for another for herself. Hermes lifted his face, scowling at his sister. "Would you please not discuss me as if I'm not here?"

Athena angled her head to the side. "What an odd notion. We are in the same room, brother. You can hear and see us, and we can see you, in turn. If I speak of you by your name instead of directly addressing you, it is because I'm speaking to Arachne and Lydia, who do not know what we know. We all need to be clear that this is not about a jealous lover, but a being that feeds on the fears and night-mares when she is not in control of her faculties."

Nora visibly shuddered. I couldn't say that the news didn't creep me out, too. Melinoë had tried to get past my defenses. I didn't need her or anyone else creeping into my secret thoughts much less my fears, and I most definitely didn't want anyone reading my more recent nightmares of losing Hermes. However, despite Melinoë's intentions terrifying me, at least she wasn't hurt by what she saw.

The god grimaced at his sister, but he seemed less distraught as well. "I see. Glad we're all cleared up here."

"Not nearly," Athena replied, her gaze on Nora. "We need a games schedule to see whom Melinoë is up against. She can tear into anyone's mind that doesn't have a strong mental defense."

"Agent Tan said we'll have the roster on day of each event," the priestess provided, taking her own coffee and settling in a chair.

That, I had missed. "So, we don't know who we're competing against until right before?"

"Correct," Athena blew on her coffee before taking a seat. "Also, we will not know what the game or challenge will be until we are in the designated area."

It was my turn to scowl. "What? We had specific sports that we picked, and everyone practiced for."

The goddess shrugged.

This turn of events did nothing to lighten my mood.

The doors opened. Rhiannon, Lance, Daystar, Princess, and some shifters walked in, followed shortly by Gabriel and Phyr. Miriam was outside the door, Thanatos hovering close to her speaking animatedly in his human-ish form. Meanwhile Lucifer glared daggers at Death. The witchy fae seemed to have picked up the Norse goddess Hel, too.

She came in. "Oh, so you've discussed how no one knows what the competitions will be."

We all nodded. "Among other things," Athena said, glancing at Hermes and me.

Phyr stretched. More than one set of eyes watched the display. He was a handsome bastard, and he knew it. A sly grin touched his lips and mischief sparkled in his eyes as his gaze set on Gabriel. "Like how Lucifer openly plans to *accidentally* kill me and Gabriel. Well, at least Gabriel. I'm not as much of a threat as a curiosity."

"So that's two competitors who definitely want a few of us dead. That's two too many," Rhiannon said and then ordered the wall dispenser, "An extra-large, triple meat pizza and two pitchers of soda." She clapped her hands with delight when the food and drinks appeared. "Magic is so cool."

"So you noticed Melinoë," I asked.

Rhiannon nodded as she handed out slices to the shifters. "Oh, yeah."

"Everyone did," Gabriel answered. "What is her beef with you?"

I gestured at Hermes. "I am engaged to her snack."

The were-nephil gave me a sympathetic smile. "Seems a problem we have in common."

"Which sucks. When a scorned lover is the issue, there is no room for negotiation," Rhiannon mused before shoving the pizza in her mouth.

"It's not about being her lover. Lydia used the term snack because I was food for Melinoë," Hermes replied. "Metaphysically speaking, that is. She addicted me to her while she fed off my fears and nightmares."

"How horrible." Miriam crossed her arms over her chest as if hugging herself. "Lucifer had addicted me to his angel dust so that I would do his bidding. I didn't know my own mind. It was so bad, I wanted to die."

I swallowed hard, staring and wondering how Miriam could even be in the same room as the king of Hell after what he did to her. How her partners could either was beyond me.

Gabriel embraced the witch fae. Phyr sidled next to them and slid an arm around Miriam as well. The latter two gave each other looks that revealed they were communicating telepathically.

I sighed and glanced at Hermes. Sometimes I could know what he was thinking, but not at the moment. Especially not after learning Melinoë fed off his mind. Telepathy would be too intrusive for him. Plus, I liked a modicum of privacy to think what I liked to think. Still a direct form of communication no one else could hear would be nice.

Hermes exhaled. "Death would only make me entirely hers. She'd trap my shade for eternity." The god waved his hand. "Melinoë's chaotic side is not like Lucifer. She is not an evil being. She takes on the madness of the shades she is warden over so there is a part of her that suffers greatly and does the awful things. She cannot help it. It is the only thing that eases the mental anguish."

Miriam touched her mouth. Several of the shifters gave him a sympathetic look. My own heart squeezed in my chest. I knew first-hand that Hermes gave all of himself to someone he loved. He'd come to my aide against the wishes of his father and at his own peril in more ways than one. *Did he ever contemplate allowing this goddess to have him to save her?*

"It's not the same, yet it is," Miriam replied. "In his mind, Lucifer did what he'd done to bring those who sided with him back to their world. He also wanted to take away the Angelic Anocracy's power over the human world."

NINETEEN

A hologram of two separate messages appeared at the foot of the bed, with the same holographic woman as we'd seen the first day standing in between. She smiled. "Any questions?"

I rubbed my eyes and nudged Hermes. The god grumbled a bit and sat up, exhaling through his nose as he read the message meant for him. "A footrace for me. I don't think this is a fair challenge."

The hologram looked at him. "Is that a question?"

"No." He threw off the covers and got out of bed. Turning, he climbed back on to kiss me. "I will see you later, victorious."

I grinned at his confidence. He was fast and could cross the interstitial space between worlds as a shortcut. So could Phyr, for that matter. Thank goodness the two planeswalkers didn't have to compete against each other. Thanatos, though, also had the ability. I hoped they both made it into the top rankings. They had their quarrels but would look out for each other if they kept getting placed in the same games.

"What is your assignment?"

Sighing, I gestured to my message. "I'm to report to the crevice. I don't know what that means."

"No need to guess," the hologram replied. "The crevice is the game."

Hermes and I exchanged a look.

"You have fifteen minutes to be at your designated areas, or you will be disqualified. Disqualification will result in immediate removal from the Vault," the AI warned.

We rolled our eyes. Hermes gave me a quick kiss. As the god shut the door to the bathroom, I got out of bed and brushed my thick curls into a ponytail. Then, I pinned the curls into a bun. The hologram stuck around. With a bobby pin in my mouth, I asked, "I have a question. Is the race Hermes will compete in dangerous?"

The hologram took a moment to respond. "Until competitions are complete, the details cannot be shared with those who do not take part."

"Sure. Right." I threw on my team uniform and left for my assignment.

The door led me to what looked like the interior of a rock-climbing facility. Except, there was no belaying equipment, nor was there an end to the two gray and tan walls in either direction. I craned my neck and couldn't make out a ceiling. There were several ledges and many cracks and crevices for hand holds. The walls ran past the point I could perceive with my eyes, and I had a harpy's vision. Calling the game "the crevice" made more sense now. Figuring the games would be like a track and field competition, I hadn't thought rock climbing would be on a list of things that we should practice for. I hoped I'd be up for the task. I had no doubt I wouldn't win the competition, but I'd at least keep my team in the running.

Black orbs whizzed about, reminding me we were being watched all over the multiverse. *Great. No pressure!*

Oberon, Hel, and some other supernaturals I recognized, walked through doors that opened seemingly out of nowhere. In reaper garb, Thanatos appeared among them. Waving skeletal fingers, he made his way over to me, face shadowed by his hooded robes.

"Well, this is not what I expected first," he grumbled in his raspy voice, the interior of his hood tilting upward as he took everything in.

"Me either."

"Do you think they want us to climb this?"

"I should hope so. I'm not down for a running with the bulls situation."

Although I couldn't quite see it, I could perceive Thanatos's smile. "Indeed."

Oberon, high king of the Unseelie fae, approached us. There was something about the way Miriam's father moved with regal grace as if he were gliding in a ballroom instead of walking the crowding space. His courtly manner set him apart from the rest despite wearing the green t-shirt and track pants provided. Or was it his bare feet and gym clothes? The few times I'd seen him, the king wore 18th century men's heeled boots and dressed in a cross between Prince and the cast of Hamilton. He bowed his pink-haired and white-antlered head ceremoniously. Glittering green eyes met mine. They were like Miriams, uncanny and fathomless in their depths. "Oracle."

"King Oberon." I curtsied. I didn't know if I did it right, but the fae king smiled his pleasure.

The king's bottle green eyes took in Thanatos. "Disappointed you couldn't be paired with my daughter?"

For once, Thanatos didn't have an immediate comeback. He made a choking sound and managed a monosyllabic affirmative.

Oberon quirked an eyebrow, shook his head as if dismissing a thought, and then asked, "Can I trust that you shall act in a manner proper for a suitor to the heir of the Unseelie throne?"

The god of death scratched the hood of his robe. "I—I'm not following."

"If you wish to be Miriam's consort, then you must..." His gaze drifted toward the place where Lucifer stood among the waiting contestants. The green eyes flicked preternaturally fast back to Thanatos. "Ensure your position."

Even I felt the weight Oberon placed on the word "ensure".

"I can't do anything to disqualify my team," the God of Death whispered. His voice lacked all the usual humor.

I didn't like it. Oberon didn't need to put more pressure on my friend. However, I kept my peace. I had enough enemies without making one that had zero moral scruples when it came to his kid...or anything else. Anyone who thought Carmen was an acceptable romantic partner scared me.

"Phyr fought in a war, gave up his rightful rule of his own faerie, his position in his family's court, and left his world to be her consort. Gabriel lost his Grace and his relationship with father and the angels is forever ruined. He would have given up his pack and his position, even his life to protect her. Pity, you think this game is worth more than my daughter's love." Oberon shrugged and turned away as if he hadn't just suggested Thanatos needed to up his game to life or death or he wasn't worthy of Miriam.

Thanatos's hood swung to me. "Did you hear that?"

I squeezed his bony shoulder in empathy, and I wasn't being metaphorical about it being bony. I felt only fabric and bones, not a scrap of flesh on his reaper form. "He's a concerned father. Not to mention, if he dies in these games, she'll rule all of the fae. Time to consider if she's worth pursuing."

As if to further my point, Hel bumped Thanatos's wing, sneering as she passed. Bold move considered he had his reaping scythe on his back. Then again, she was a goddess of a different underworld. It might have no effect on her.

The god's exhale sounded like bone scraping bone and defeat. The hood of his robe followed the Norse goddess making her way through the contestants. When she was out of earshot, he remarked,

"She's worth it. The question is whether I will survive with so many other people after her."

I pointed at Hel doing the same shoulder bump to Lucifer. The king of Hell's pearl clutching, gaping mouth reaction made me giggle a bit. "Well, at least you're not the only one disliked for your romantic interest in her."

"Yeah." Thanatos chuckled, a dry, raspy sound. Sobering, he asked, "How about we watch each other's back for this game?"

I grinned at Death. "There's nothing in the rules against contestants teaming up."

A hologram of Agent Tan's face appeared above between the two walls. "The goal of this event is to find a golden egg touched by King Midas himself. You must use both your physical abilities and magical senses to detect whether the golden egg you find is simply natural gold or transmogrified by Midas. Those with wings or levitation abilities won't be able to fly their way to the top. However, you won't be disqualified for flying as needed. The only way to be disqualified from the actual game is to die or kill someone."

"Glad they clarified dying would disqualify you at the same time mentioning killing will as well."

Some supernaturals began climbing.

"Are we supposed to start?" Thanatos asked.

I took off my shoes. Pain seared through my back as I released my wings. Talons formed on hands and feet. "Yeah. I think so."

Eyeing my wings and talons, Thanatos remarked, "Guess it's good to be you, Big Bird."

The image of the yellow Sesame Street came to mind. "Um. Don't call me th——-" The words drowned in the thundering of hooves.

"Stampede!" someone cried.

I took flight, only to slam into and ricochet off an unseen force. "Damn it."

"Flying isn't an option." Thanatos held out a hand. I took it.

The noise of the incoming stampede and the contestants scrambling to get out of the way rang in my ears as I clambered up the façade as far and as fast as I could. When I got far enough to be safely above the chaos below, I peered down. A deluge of brown bulls poured across the crevice floor. They weren't exactly bulls, but rather a hybrid bull-man, running on humanoid powerful legs.

"Minotaurs?"

"Doesn't matter. The floor is lava, Lydia. That's all we need to know," Thanatos called from above.

His robe had fallen away or simply disappeared in the chaos. The god of death now wore his team's grey shirt and sweats. His wings were gone, and his scythe had shrunk to a much smaller size on his back, but still visible, leaving me to wonder why he wore it at all. Thanatos could place it in a pocket realm and pull it out at will, even make the scythe the size of a toothpick and hold it in his mouth if he wanted.

"Noted."

The climb wasn't easy, especially with other supes nearby. We soon spread out, or the wall grew and spaced us. I wasn't sure which. Like Miriam's faerie, this place didn't follow Earth rules. I scanned my surroundings. Soon, we reached a ledge that was out of view from the floor. Thanatos and I sat scanning the view. Not only hidden ledges lined the wall opposite ours, but caves dotted the wall, too. I wondered how the game makers had made an entire climbing facility that high.

"What if the egg is over there?" I asked, nodding to the opposite wall.

He eyed my wings. "Use those and I'll use mine."

"Can't." I grimaced and admitted, "I tried flying to escape the minotaurs. Hit a barrier of some sort."

"Hmmm..." Thanatos stroked his chin. "She said we can fly as needed. Maybe that means we can fly to and from the opposite side, or if we fall, but not directly up?"

"That would be a silly rule."

The god shrugged thin shoulders. "Evening the odds?"

"Not everyone can fly back and forth." To emphasize my point, I gestured to the wingless contestants. We all seemed even further apart and so did the walls, which tied an anxious knot in my gut. How were we supposed to find the egg if the walls grew?

"Supernaturals don't need wings. They'll find a way to use their magic. We won't be the only ones teaming up, either." He clambered to his feet and started climbing. "We won't find anything if we stay put."

The God of Death had a point, we were the only ones within sight sitting still. However, I remained where I was. Tan said that there would be proof of the transmogrification. All magic had a signature color.

"Show me where you are, golden egg," I whispered.

Using my second sight that could detect the color of magic, I took in a sweeping view of the opposite wall. Several places higher up on the opposite wall lit up. To test Thanatos's theory, I decided to fly over to the cave opposite. It was not directly opposite, but on the same level as the ledge where I'd rested.

"Hey," Thanatos cried out as I leapt forward, spreading my wings.

Ignoring him I kept my eyes on the tiny pinprick of yellow light in the cave. I'd grown somewhat adept at flying and managed to stay relatively at the same height as my former perch. I could fall to my demise, though. If I strayed even a little bit higher than I'd been, I'd hit a barrier and dip down pretty far. Too far. I almost grazed my foot on a milling minotaur's horn. The creature bellowed a cry that sounded eerily like a human's angry shout, yet that of a bull. I shuddered inwardly, beating my wings to escape the enraged monster's wrath. Upon brief observation, the minotaurs seemed confused and angry rather than murderous. I couldn't consider their plight now. I had to reach the cave. The other contestants had reached so high up, I could hardly see them. Preternatural speed and agility made fast work, but my bet is that some had started exploring the caves.

Something caught my eye as I ascended, a tiny magenta spark. I almost carried on to my original destination. However, maybe, it was my imagination, but the light blinked as if signaling me. I'd take it as a trick of the eye but the blinking continued. I hovered there a moment, then had an *Aha!* moment.

All the other lights I'd seen were yellow. My heart raced. Yellow or white was the color of witchlight. I'd seen it many times in the Gonzalez family spellwork. So, the magical source in the cave above had come from a witch. When Apollo had cursed my friend Lucky Joey, the light had been magenta—the color of gods' magic. According to the story my grandparents had told me, Midas hadn't been a witch, but he'd received his golden touch from Dionysus, one of the Twelve.

I nose dove toward the cave, pausing only to turn my attention to the sound of wingbeats above. It took all my will not to shriek in horror. The God of Death's reaper form in a tracksuit was a skeletal nightmare with wings.

I bit my lip to hide the blood curdling fear I'd betray in my voice, and I pointed to the cave. Thanatos followed me to the small ledge before what was no more than a crevice. Funny. The cave had seemed...well, a cave, before.

"I guess I can scratch off scaring the Oracle speechless to my bucket list," Thanatos said with a curve of his skeletal mouth, giving me no small amount of the heebie-jeebies.

Shaking off my ick, I knelt, reached inside the dark space, and snatched the golden egg with a magenta aura. The metal felt smooth and cool nestled in the palm of my hand.

Thanatos's skeletal face managed to look worried. Skeletor had nothing on the God of Death for emoting with bones. "This was too easy, Lydia."

I didn't disagree. "What now?"

"With the bull boys downstairs." He pointed a skeletal finger to the seemingly never-ending darkness above. "There's only one way out."

I stuffed the egg down my shirt, nestling it between my breasts.

"That's one place to put it," Thanatos quipped. "How about we use old faithful." He patted his scythe.

I handed him the egg, trusting that even if he stole it and ran, I would at least survive this round to make it to the next one.

He tapped the egg with the scythe, sucking it into wherever the god stored shades or whatever.

With that settled, we began our ascent. For what seemed like an eternity, we climbed the wall. Eventually, we caught up to the other contestants clambering, scaling, and checking for eggs.

"Should we pretend to look?" I asked Thanatos in a barely audible whisper.

He nodded.

Pretending to look made the ascent even harder. We had to spend time exploring crevices and caves. Resting here and there. I was thirsty, hungry, and tired.

Winged supernaturals learned the hard way they couldn't fly past certain points. Still, a supernatural with a human head and brown and grey speckled feathered body flew straight up at full speed. A birdish screech escaped the supe as she bounced off the barrier, ricocheting down at the same velocity. I couldn't bear to watch the descent, keeping my eyes on the goal above.

I didn't hear the crash, but a series of loud, bullish bellows echoed from below. Thanatos paused and then shook his head. "The Uchek Langmeidong's team is out."

Confirming the death, a bell tolled. I closed my eyes. It was the first game, and someone had already died. I didn't have time to mourn the stranger or consider my part in their death for long. A jewel-scaled serpent with diaphanous wings glided past us, sniffing. Unfamiliar, cold magic probed at my mental shields, slithering along my defenses. I held my breath and reinforced the protective layer in my mind.

"No sniffing out secrets from me, asshole," I muttered and continued up the side.

After flying too close for comfort for several fluttering heartbeats, the dragon moved on.

By the time Thanatos and I reached the very top of the wall, my muscles ached, and I thought I couldn't climb another inch. I didn't bother to stand. I laid motionless and eyes closed for several panting breaths.

"Fancy meeting you here," Thanatos quipped in his raspy voice, but I knew him well enough to hear an underlying tone of apprehension.

When I opened my eyes, a tall, muscular woman with curling dark hair and olive skin stared back at me with the cold, calculating eyes of a predator. I swallowed hard, considering my current options, and really wished disappearing like a planeswalker was one of them.

I wasn't intimidated by the hard stare but rather that she had a bow and arrow. The specific trouble I had with that was that the arrow was notched, and the bow drawn. All the goddess had to do was let go. My heart would have a hard time beating with a shaft through it.

Trembling inside, I waved and smiled. "Oh, hey Artemis."

The goddess didn't have her twin brother's easy smile. Her beautiful face could be carved from stone for all the emotion she expressed. "Give me the egg."

I held up both hands. "Don't have one. We were going to look up here."

"Liar!"

Yes. I was a liar. However, this liar had enough time to gather up lightning from the static in the air. I sent a bolt right up her arm, burning the arrow and bow. The goddess shook. Her eyes rolled back. For a minute I thought that she'd pull through the attack and counterattack. Instead, the imposing beauty slumped to the ground.

I got up and checked her pulse. She wasn't dead, but Artemis would be down for a while.

"Shit," Thanatos said, rubbing his now human-looking forehead. "You've gained more control than anyone in the Underworld heard."

"The harpies don't rat on their queens. We'd better find a way out before we run into more trouble."

The god pointed to an object in the distance. "Are those scales?"

I squinted. "Yup. I bet they can tell whether an egg is transmogrified or not."

Sphere drones gathered and hovered near as we sprinted over. The scales sat upon a marble doric column. The scale itself had a small stone on one side and a gleaming empty golden tray on the other.

Thanatos retrieved the egg from who knows where and handed it to me. "You should have the honor since you're the one who found it."

I grinned and nodded my thanks. My hand trembled as I sat the egg on the scale's tray. Part of me envisioned trap doors opening beneath my feet and Thanatos stepping away and laughing maniacally. Thankfully, it was an intrusive thought, not a prophetic vision.

A tingling bell rang. Then horns blasted so loud I had to cover my ears. Fireworks went off. A holograph banner flew in the sky. It read, "Red team wins!"

The electric tingle of magic coursed through me, giving me a high like I'd drank a thousand cups of coffee, had the best sex ever, and the certainty I could conquer anything. My minor cuts and bruises from the challenge stopped hurting.

Thanatos gasped, holding up his hands. His eyes glowed magenta. The same light limned his skeletal fingers.

Looking at my own hands, I gaped. The same magenta light tinged with other colors limned my fingers. My gaze swung back to the God of Death. My own wariness somehow reflected in the shadows of his hood.

Before Thanatos and I could discuss what was happening to us, a holographic image of Agent Tan appeared. She was joined by Agents Doyle and Roanhorse. All three wore black suits and solemn expressions. A corner of Tan's mouth ticked up as she took in me and Thanatos.

"Congratulations, Lydia Kourakos from team red. You found Midas's transmogrified egg. You've won."

Doors appeared.

"I guess we're meant to leave now," Thanatos said, his raspy voice warbling with emotion.

I glanced over my shoulder at the crevice. "Yeah. No time to let hard feelings set in."

CHAPTER

TWENTY

I stood in front of the wall dispenser in the common room for the red team, waiting for a glass of water to drink with my cooling plate of moussaka. The water sloshed in the glass as I carried it to the table. My room had been empty and so was the common room. I'd already taken a shower and changed into my loungewear from home. Worry gnawed at my insides, keeping me from any sort of rest and recuperation from the days' events. If I wasn't famished from the arduous climb, I doubt I could have eaten. However, my hands clumsily handled my food. It took three tries before I could get a bite of the eggplant dish in my mouth.

Phyr appeared seemingly out of thin air. He staggered and fell into a chair, his chest heaving with his labored breaths. Blood seeped multiple tears in his armor and flesh. It appeared that some taloned beast had nearly torn him to shreds. His eyes and the swirling script glowed green, illuminating his bronze skin.

Meal forgotten, I rushed to his side. "Do you need—"

The fae cut me off with wave of his hand and demanded, "Accora Tati?"

"Um, I don't speak Unseelie."

Thick slashes of eyebrows knitted together as he panted. He'd said something he hadn't meant to. That would have revealed just how badly he'd been injured, even if I couldn't see the white of bone where his sternum should be. I hated that I'd seen enough gore from previous battles that the sight only made me feel slightly nauseated.

Looking wildly about, Phyr asked in a desperate tone, "Where is Miriam?"

I threw up my hands. My own worry conveyed in the gesture. "No one has come back yet, or at least not here. Wait. Don't you two have a bond that you can communicate through?"

His lips twisted in a snarl—a look I've never seen on him before. The snarl faded and his shoulders slumped. He covered his face and in a bleak tone admitted, "We do. However, I couldn't feel her the moment I entered the competition. Nothing. Nothing should be able to do that." In a quieter tone, he said, "Not even death. Not a bond like ours."

The Vault was powerful enough to sever a fae mate bond.

"I'm sorry." I meant it. It had to be maddening to go from constant connection to nothing. An idea occurred to me. Everything was being recorded. "Assistant, can we watch the games from here?" I asked, hoping the hologram would appear.

Within a blink she appeared with a smile that disconcerted me, given how badly Phyr was still injured. "Which of the games would you like to watch?"

Before I could reply, Phyr ordered, "Show me Miriam."

A holographic screen appeared, displaying a body of water rippling in a facsimile of moonlight. The angle of the view suggested the camera drone took the shot from above, closing in on an antlered woman with eyes that illuminated. At the sight of his lover, Phyr breathed out a sigh of relief. However, his relief was short lived as he watched the events unfold. The fae prince leaned forward, watching the witchy fae princess swim, or rather, treading water with one hand while holding a large plume above the waves with the other. Her eyes illuminated the water ahead of her with green fae light. A dark shadow swam not far behind her. The camera zoomed in on the face of that shadow, giving it more light than the contestants were allowed. Despite her hair being soaked and the lighting on her much dimmer, I recognized the dark-haired beauty. You never forgot someone like her, someone as beautiful as they were lethal.

I gestured to the holographic image. "At least Carmen is with her."

Without taking his eyes off Miriam, Phyr replied, "That wolf shifter's presence, dear child of Olympus, is not at all comforting. They're competing against each other, remember?"

"Thanatos and I allied, during our competition."

Phyr gestured to his slowly healing wounds. "Melinoë did not extend me the same spirit of generosity." A hint of the prince I knew returned as he added, "The goddess appeared to be greatly disappointed she couldn't invade my mind and make me her puppet like the others."

A modicum of relief loosened the knot of worry in my chest. Hermes and Melinoë hadn't been in the same competition. I then processed what he'd said. "She took over people's minds?"

"It's allowed, apparently." Bitterness laced his tone.

"Oh my, how did you escape?"

"Fortunately, I have the same ability, remember?"

I shuddered, remembering the way he made mundanes into puppets. The fact he and Miriam could do that gave me new appreciation they were on my side.

"Our competition became a matter of wills. She is young and a novice. I am younger, but more experienced." He spared a glance from Miriam's game to wink at me. That was a good sign the prince was feeling somewhat better.

Assessing him, I noticed some of his wounds had closed and others were getting there.

His gaze returned the screen, our conversation forgotten. Carmen stuck so close she might be giving chase, or they'd definitely teamed up.

"She is Oberon's consort. She's going to help his daughter." I didn't know if I was easing his mind or my own since I was also sitting at the edge of my seat.

"You think like a human, Oracle."

I shrugged. "I still think of myself as human. A supernatural one, but human nonetheless, so I don't take that as an insult, but please elaborate why you think Carmen won't help Miriam."

"The high king confided in Miriam that his consort wants to have his children."

"What does that have to do with the games?"

He rolled his eyes but didn't spare me another glance. "Miriam is heir. That weakens Carmen and her future children's position in court. Shifters are powerful predators, but their mothers don't have protective spells like witches and fae. To preserve their mother's honor and eliminate the competition for the throne, Maeve and Nix will have no qualms murdering their half siblings in infancy. She won't kill Miriam directly, but she will make sure that she dies."

"I'm still not following."

"If she opens a path for Maeve or Nix to be named heir, Carmen will guarantee safety of her future children and her position in court. Not to mention she'd make a powerful alpha among the shifters. Miriam and Gabriel out of the way would ensure possible mates for the fae nobility looking for a highly fertile, magical, but short-lived mate. Also, without their interference, she'd have the added benefit of taking her current children back from Princess and Aurora."

I wrung my hands watching Miriam swim and cheering her on in my head. "Supernatural politics are awful."

Phyr exhaled a loud, long-suffering sigh. "Why do you think I wish to be a simple baker?"

"As long as you're a fae mate bonded with the heir to the Unseelie throne, that'll never be true, Phyr." I grinned. He might say he wanted to be a baker, but that prince was born a prince not an ignoramus who signed her name in blood to get away from the cops. Phyr had known what bonding with her meant.

"I knew that I would never be a simple anything the moment she whispered her true name in my ear." There was wistfulness to his tone. He grinned back even though he didn't look in my direction. "However, I am the most fortunate fae to ever walk the planes to be her chosen."

We both turned our attention to the events unfolding on screen. Neither woman looked happy. Carmen kept pausing to look behind them. The camera panned to two dark figures in the distance heading their way.

It was hard to see that Miriam had ended up in no better circumstances than I'd been in—perhaps worse. A niggling voice said that I'd put her in this situation. I pushed that voice right out of my head. Everyone had volunteered to compete in these games.

Miriam kept the feather above her head and swam at a steady pace despite only using one arm. Her eyes glowed green, illuminating the water like headlights. Carmen slowed, shouting in Miriam's direction, "Keep going!"

The fae-witch hesitated, looking back at the same figures that had paused Carmen.

Phyr sprang to his feet. "No! That murderous mutt isn't worth a single hair on your head, anam cara."

Miriam spoke in a language I didn't understand. The water churned and swallowed the shadowy figures. "That'll hold them under for a bit."

Carmen's responding grin gleamed with malice. "You're just like your father."

Something unreadable passed over Miriam's face, there and gone. Given Oberon was a murderous fae king, I doubted his daughter liked the comparison.

She and Carmen continued, climbing onto a rocky shore. Both women had slashes, bite marks, and what looked like burns on their bodies. Miriam seemed to be better off than Carmen but both would heal. They sprinted around the island until they came upon a set of scales, not exactly like the one that I'd placed the egg on but similar in style.

"The Feather of Ma'at," Miriam announced, placing the feather on the scale.

WINNER! flashed on the hologram. Fireworks went off in the night sky, reflected in the water. Again, the agents showed up, Roanhorse announcing the winner.

Eventually, all of team red returned, some more worse for the wear than others. Most grabbed food and returned to their quarters, their eyes haunted. Many were visibly shaken. I pushed down the guilt that bubbled up with each appearance. Everyone here had volunteered. Also, every time someone showed, I hoped Hermes would walk through. So far, my hopes had been dashed. I couldn't bring myself to watch him compete. Unlike Phyr and Miriam, who watched Gabriel.

The nephil shifter had it rough. The game was a hunt for a unicorn and the unicorn had to be brought back alive. To my surprise, he'd ended up teaming up with a Fallen angel. Not to my surprise the Fallen double-crossed him and tried to take the unicorn for themself. The two faced an angel, who'd paired up with another being I could not name. While the four battled for the unicorn, an Unseelie fae I didn't recognize and a god from the Norse pantheon, perhaps Fenrir, stole the magical beast and won. Gabriel had a nasty attitude when he returned. Phyr made him something to eat and Miriam tended to his wounds.

I continued to wait for Hermes.

Arachne's children carried her through. My monster friend appeared haggard, much older and less cheerful than when she sat with her knitting needles in our kitchen in Milagro Bay.

"Okay, we're safe. You can let me walk on my own now," she griped, scrambling to her feet. Her children surrounded her as she skittered and plopped onto a round chair that seemed made for her unusual proportions.

I got her something to eat to distract myself from Hermes still not making an appearance.

The elderly monster glanced around the room. Her watery brown eyes filled with concern. "Has Athena come back yet? I was hoping she'd already be here."

With a rueful smile, I shook my head and sat in a chair next to her, letting myself sink deep into the cushions with a sigh. "Neither has Hermes."

Arachne took a bite out of her burrito and placed a hand over mine. She said around a mouthful of food, "You have good reason to be worried. He's fast and powerful, but there's bloodlust and vain-glory idiots going around a plenty."

My challenge seemed tame compared to what Miriam, Phyr, and Arachne went through. Hermes might be in a battle to the death right now. I shuddered at the thought. "I don't understand why anyone would want to look like the bad guy when the games are public."

"That was nothing like an Olympic game. What happened there will never leave me. A bloodbath of supernaturals that I haven't seen since the days when we warred in the past. They can't kill anyone, and supes don't die easily, but they sure as heck came close."

Cold dread formed in the pit of my stomach. Changing the subject, I asked, "Did you win?"

A grin briefly lit her weathered features. "No one dislikes me, so I was able to manage the labyrinth with little problem." She beamed down proudly at the bowling ball sized spiders crawling up her skirt. Still, her eyes held sadness. "My children were quick and quiet, stealing the object of power while the others fought. We won through our cunning."

I made a mental note that stealing the prize was an option. However, I didn't want to win. I wanted to survive, not gain power... didn't I?

"I can feel it," she said, breaking me from my thoughts.

"Feel what?"

"Power coursing through me. More than I ever felt. My win mattered."

"I'd felt something, too—I hadn't expected that."

She scowled. "Why not? That's what everyone here is after. Why they're willing to risk everything. Why the angelic anocracy fought the fae. Why Lucifer wanted to use Miriam to destroy Earth. Belief is the most powerful magic of all."

CHAPTER

TWENTY-ONE

Nora came through next. After a brief once-over of her body, I couldn't find a scratch on her. Yet, her eyes were wild, and her hands shook as I gave her some water and something to eat at the common room's table. She didn't speak at first. It took some coaxing to get her to sip the water and take a spoonful or two of avgolemono, her favorite Greek soup that I usually made back in my kitchen. She ate the soup and drank robotically, only pausing to push her braids behind her shoulders.

Arachne and I exchanged a worried glance. The priestess wasn't a chatty Cathy, but she usually spoke more than this. We let her eat in peace.

Finally, Nora spoke, "If it weren't for Cosmo's protection, we wouldn't have won. I wouldn't be alive."

"He's a good seaman, that Cosmo." I smiled and wrapped an arm around her shoulders, grateful that Poseidon's general had come through for my friend. "I'm glad you made it."

"There's a price to winning." She lifted her hand. It was just a brown hand on a lovely priestess, but I guessed she was reliving that moment when belief hit her. "I'm not human anymore. I can feel it."

133

Arachne scoffed. "Nonsense! Nothing can take your humanity, not magic, not wings. You are who you are."

Nora nodded, but I could see in her features she didn't believe it.

"Do you think of me as not human?" I swallowed hard. My fear of what she'd reply reflected in my voice. Maybe she thought of me as a monster. I did sprout wings and talons now and then, after all.

Her deep brown eyes seemed to see me for the first time since she arrived. "Of course you're human."

I didn't know why but her answer mattered. "Being human isn't what you look like or your magical ability or not. We can have children with other humans. We can love like a human. Everything else is just a bonus."

Her brows knitted together. "Does that mean that all gods and monsters who can do those things have a bit of humanity in them?"

I shrugged. "That's not up to them, and not for me to decide."

"I am victorious," Athena's voice boomed as if on loudspeaker.

The debate was immediately forgotten as we took in her appearance. Blood and other gore covered her grim face, hair, and team clothes. A magenta aura limned her body and her eyes glowed like high beams. She held her Aegis with a screaming facsimile of Medusa's head in one hand and a bloody spear in the other.

Arachne skittered over, embracing the goddess. Athena rested her forehead on Arachne's, whispering something low and soothing to her tearful partner.

Nora shyly crossed the room, wringing her hands. Clearly, she wanted to embrace Athena, too, but did not interrupt the reunion.

Arachne opened her arms. "Come here, you."

Athena made space for her priestess. Nora didn't move as the goddess's gaze swept the length of her, assessing. The normally stoic Athena released a chest-heaving sigh of relief. It didn't last. Her eyes narrowed shrewdly. "You have gained more magic than I have bestowed upon you."

Curious, I tilted my head to the side. No one had told me that Athena had gifted Nora. I knew from legends like Midas that the gods could imbue mundanes with magic, but I hadn't ever experienced it.

Nora licked her lips. "Yes. I—I still serve you."

Cupping Nora's cheek, Athena smiled. The brilliant flash of teeth happened so seldomly compared to her brother Hermes, and she was not her aunt Aphrodite or her sister Persephone in terms of beauty, but Athena's smile of approval was a rare and precious gift. "I am glad you have your own power Nike Nora Jones. Your bravery and willingness to represent your world is worthy of such a reward. However, your indomitable spirit is the fountain from which magic springs forth. I only found what was within you and so did those who saw you today."

The priestess's face beamed and there wasn't a dry eye in the room as she embraced Athena. I longed to join them, but it wasn't my moment. Even Arachne backed away, excusing herself. After a long, long embrace, Athena and Nora separated.

The goddess turned her gaze to me. "You are well and are more powerful, too," she stated, adding, "We have much to discuss."

"We do," I agreed.

"First, I will cleanse myself of Hera and other's blood."

I eyed the gore. "Good idea."

After a shower and change of clothes, Athena settled at the table in a fresh, red jumpsuit. At her request, Arachne brought her some of the same soup that Nora had been eating and some pita. She began eating but it was slow going as she and Nora explained their competition. They'd both been in obstacle course type of settings where they had to use magic and other means to find objects of power. Athena said that her competition turned into just how far the competitors could injure each other with traps and then a brawl happened at the end.

Zeus, Demeter, and Hestia returned in the meantime. With each new arrival, my heart lurched in my chest, hoping it would be Hermes. They all shared their harrowing stories.

The former king of the gods grinned. "Poseidon, Aidoneus, and I were unstoppable."

Demeter swallowed her wine. "As bad as it was, it was so nice to be in the same game as Persephone."

"I got to be with a lovely and fierce siren named Lucinda," Hestia agreed.

"How wonderful," Athena replied dryly. "Hera stabbed me in the shoulder. She wanted me to know it could've been my heart. I have never been an object of my stepmother's vengeance or jealousy. That she harmed my person for power pained me, and it pained me more to beat her to a bloody pulp, leaving just enough ichor in her to not disqualify myself."

Not quite able to grasp this side of Athena, Nora stared in horror. Arachne busied herself with cleanup and got her to help. I just listened. I knew the goddess had a temper.

Zeus squeezed his daughter's hand. "I'm sorry it's come to this."

Athena withdrew from him and defiantly lifted her chin. "If you'd acted after Amphitrite's attack on Milagro Bay, we'd not be here."

The former king of the gods looked to me for assistance. As much as I didn't want to get involved, I had made the prediction that if he'd acted, he'd start a war he couldn't finish. I spread my hands. "The threads didn't read that way, Athena."

"I know. I've heard your prophecy. I've heard all the prophecies." She pushed to her feet. "Prophecies have destroyed this family."

Demeter opened her mouth and closed it. Her brow furrowed in consternation, but she eventually looked at her hands. Hestia shrunk in her chair. If a black hole opened behind her, I had no doubt she'd allow herself to be swallowed whole.

Hermes stumbled into the team room. He was bleeding from a gash on his forehead, his nose was bruised and more blood trickled from it, something green and tuberous protruded from his shoulder, and the god had several more lacerations and contusions covering his body than had been on Phyr when he had returned. His eyes met mine. Relief washed over his battered features before he collapsed.

TWENTY-TWO

For what might have been seconds or full minutes, my mind believed that the nightmares which had plagued me for so long finally had come to fruition. Without a doubt, I was certain Hermes had died. A wail escaped my lips. A voice inside me rallied.

Get up! Get up! Get up!

Snapping out of my grief, I scrambled to his rescue. Athena and Arachne, who must've also experienced a state of shock, followed almost as fast. Drone spheres appeared, hovering above. Their presence here wasn't a good sign. To add to my growing fears, the thing protruding from his back wriggled as if alive. I called upon the lightning, ready to kill whatever was attacking him.

"Lydia, don't," Athena warned, placing a firm grip on my shoulder. With her other hand, she gestured. "Look. His wounds aren't healing."

Indeed, the blood was still flowing and the wounds stayed open. I'd seen enough injuries from supernaturals coming back from the competition to know this wasn't normal for a god. Still, the body of the wiggling worm-like creature flexed and released. Sucking noises coming from the little monster made my stomach lurch. Sickened and unable to watch without acting, I cocked my head to the side look at the goddess. "It's alive and actively feeding on him."

"I know, but killing the creature might make things worse. We don't know if it is keeping him alive with some sort of stabilizing venom while another magical or biological agent might be at work to keep him from healing. We should seek the advice of someone who would know if it's doing more than feeding before destroying it."

Of course the goddess of wisdom was right. I grimaced anyway. Seeing Hermes in this condition and not killing the thing didn't sit well with me, but Athena's council was the wiser course of action.

"I'll get Miriam. She's the best healer we've got our team," Arachne offered.

Agreeing and trusting the witchy fae princess, I nodded.

Within moments, Miriam, Rhiannon, and the sister witches Ezmal and Frizma arrived. The additional witches had aided me in the search for Luke. However, Hermes had strong feelings regarding the Baba Yaga coven because they'd destroyed the world they were from. Many innocents lost their lives as well as the tyrannical sect of witches called warlocks the sister had set out to stop. However, Hermes was in no shape to deny their assistance, and I would refuse no one who could possibly help my lover live.

Athena shifted out of my way, but I remained next to Hermes, holding his hand. Miriam knelt at my side. Her voice gentle as she said, "I can't see where your light ends and his begins when you two are close."

I pushed to my feet and backed out of the way, allowing the witches to examine him. A drone hovered near my face and then flew over to the crowding witches. Resentment welled up. This was no moment to capture for an audience. Yet, all of it was. I could only hope that more people watching wished for his recovery than the skeptics who believed he was dead. With the fervor of a saint, I prayed for the first to be true. I'd take any help of whatever ascended gods who would listen.

Miriam and the other witches took a slow assessment, discussing the wounds and the creature in a language that tickled my ears and grazed my skin as if the words themselves contained power. It seemed to be decided that Miriam would try healing him with her own light as she had for Gabriel.

The Unseelie princess's eyes glowed green with fae light as she touched Hermes's temples. After a few moments, she shook her head. Her face was bleak when she looked at me. "Something is acting against my light. My guess is that it's the worm." Her voice cracked as she spoke. Her daughter Jada had been in a similar situation a few years ago after being stung by a manticore. She turned to the other witches. "What do you think it is? Have you seen anything like this?"

Ezmal and Frizma had a contentious back and forth in their native tongue that felt as uncomfortable as it sounded.

Athena and I exchanged glances. The goddess only expressed her usual stoicism except in the tiniest of creases between her brows, which scared me. I'd never seen Hermes's sister actually worried.

Rhiannon ended the disagreement with words that soothed like a warm bath. Ezmal shrugged and replied. Frizma folded her arms across her chest. A hint of smugness touched the corners of her mouth. Ezmal rolled her eyes as she faced me and Athena.

"We do not know this creature," Ezmal said in heavily accented English. Her words had the slow and intentional cadence of someone who thought in their first language and then expressed themselves in another tongue out loud. "However, my sister thinks the worm is keeping from healing and I believe that Athena is right. Frizma wants to remove the whole worm and see what happens. I say we cut off a piece of its tail and have I.S.E.A's forensic team analyze what type of being the little worm might be and any magical toxins it is releasing into Hermes's system. My lovely daughter-in-law suggested that we let you make the choice."

My stomach sank with the weight of the decision. No matter

what I did, Hermes could die. It felt like picking which poison to end him with.

"If I may," Miriam said, looking at a drone. "If I.S.E.A consulted with Inez Gonzalez, she would no doubt be able to identify a creature even I don't recognize. Her extensive library might even contain information on counter spells or potions that could provide the antidote without risking further damage by experimental means."

Athena voiced the same concern that rose in my own mind. "My brother could perish before that is accomplished."

The witchy fae held up her hands. "I understand your concern. However, there's a spell that could put Hermes and the worm in state of neither life nor death. I think in this state it may be possible to remove the worm and dissect it for study without harm coming to Hermes."

Ezma stepped forward. "Unless the stasis spell is broken, then he will die. Or, if the worm dies and it needs to be alive to secrete something keeping him alive. There are too many variables, and I don't like it."

"What other choice do we have?" I asked, not liking it either.

"You could read his weave," Athena suggested.

Something I'd contemplated doing many times when I experienced the nightmares of his death. Every time I was tempted to do so, I thought about other personal readings where one thread would outshine the others. When examining the threads there was a good possibility that Hermes's death could be the one most likely to happen. I didn't want his death in the hands of the Moirai. Especially when I'd agreed to replace them so Apollo would participate in the games.

Waving my hand dismissively, I refused, "No. Looking at his thread can unintentionally affect the outcome negatively. Let's do this without the weave."

"Wise." Athena nodded solemnly. "My brother would want his intended bride to decide, but I give you my approval regardless."

Hermes lay still but for the rise and fall of his chest as he took shallow breaths. I wrung my hands. Since when did his life become something for me to decide? It seemed only a short time ago we'd been strangers. At least, he'd been a stranger to me. On the other hand, as my guardian, he'd always known me. If Athena allowed me the decision because she believed Hermes also would want me to decide, then it had to be true, right?

I closed my eyes. The worst had happened. Hermes's life hung in the balance. The only two options from here were to save him or to let whatever was happening to him take its course. I wasn't ready to do the latter. However, how long would I allow him to remain in a state of not quite alive but not dead either? That would be a problem for future Lydia. For now, I made my choice. I bent over, kissing him softly on the lips, determined this was not our last kiss. We would not say goodbye.

"You will live, and we will have our wedding." The binding magic of the whispered words wrapped my body like a warm blanket and settled into my flesh marrying with all the love I felt and the intention I set burning in my chest. To Miriam and the other witches, I said, "Go ahead."

Miriam gave me a rueful smile. "Alright then."

"Wait," a familiar voice called.

A hologram of Agents Tan and Roanhorse, accompanied by Archimage Doyle, appeared. Tan and Roanhorse wore dark suits. Doyle donned gray mage's robes. All three wore solemn faces. His gaze swept to Miriam and then Rhiannon. The three exchanged a look that I couldn't read. There was something between the three of them, especially Miriam and Doyle. I wasn't certain if whatever they had was beef or a friendly tie.

Then Archimage Doyle nodded at Agent Tan. With a grimace in Hermes's direction, he said, "We've watched what happened both during the race and your handling of the situation afterward. The whole world has."

My pulse thrummed in my ears.

"I fail to see why you're interrupting me. This is a life-or-death situation." Miriam asked, arching a pink eyebrow. The witch sat a little more upright and her voice had the same imperious tone Oberon used. We were looking at the heir to the Unseelie throne, and her uncanny, green gaze set on Archimage Doyle, not Tan. "We're trying to decide if you put Hermes in stasis whether that counts as death, disqualifying the red team," Roanhorse replied.

My stomach flipped. I exchanged a worried glance with Arachne. Athena remained stone faced, yet she had the reply none of us could manage. "If you disqualify someone for dying from wounds, you must also disqualify those who dealt them."

"That's the rub." Roanhorse sighed. Uncharacteristically, the agent emoted his feelings. His expression revealed he wanted to disqualify everyone who did this to Hermes, but something was tying his hands. The agent clearly didn't like not serving justice when justice was due. "The contestants all have claimed they'd dealt wounds that are not fatal to a god—well, under normal circumstances." His dark eyed gaze narrowed on the worm and a muscle in his cheek feathered. "If the creature, which we believe is part of the Vault, is keeping him from healing, no one will be at fault.

"He will have died from conditions of the competition, I'm afraid," Archimage Doyle added.

Anger rose at the unfairness of it all. If Hermes died, every last person who harmed him would be at fault whether I.S.E.A deemed it so or not. I would personally hunt them down.

"Turn the high beams off, Oracle. It's not a good look and the whole world's watching," Agent Tan warned in her Bostonian accent.

Roanhorse added, "You can put Hermes under this stasis spell, but you've got forty-eight hours to figure out how to fix him before his next competition, or else the red team forfeits for lack of participation."

Emotions warred in my chest. Hermes would have to compete again after living through that, or else we'd be disqualified because a bunch of supes took stabs at him, and some monster decided to latch on. I swallowed my feelings down. Saving Hermes took precedence over what he'd have to face in the future.

My magic must've dimmed in my eyes because Tan smirked. "That's better."

"From what we witnessed, the creature wasn't associated with any of the contestants, but we need to be sure and also we need to be certain the creature is blocking him from healing and not some other agent," Roanhorse said.

Archimage Doyle added, "I.S.E.A Forensics is in contact with Inez and Gustavo Gonzalez. We will have Agent Maria Gonzalez personally retrieve what you're calling a worm for analysis by our lab in conjunction with the witches of Milagro Bay."

CHAPTER

TWENTY-THREE

Once the agents left, the witches started work on Hermes. They used a levitation spell to place him on a bed provided by the Vault's hologram in our shared quarters. From that point, Hermes didn't breathe, and his heart didn't beat. I wanted Thanatos to come in and tell me that Hermes was still alive. However, for everyone's safety, I.S.E.A had made it a rule that members of other teams weren't allowed to enter the common spaces or rooms of the other contestants.

After the spell was complete, the witches went about removing the worm. Even though, since taking the mantle of Oracle, I'd seen a lot more than my fair share of death and gore, I couldn't watch Frizma and Ezmal perform the combination of magical and physical surgery on Hermes. Neither could Athena. Nora and Arachne stayed to assist.

Apparently, the other supernaturals on our team were watching the other competitions, and their room AI asked if they wanted to keep abreast of their teammate's condition. They'd witnessed everything and had come to the common room to discuss. So, when Athena and I showed up, a hush spread across the room.

Zeus pushed to his feet. Arms outstretched, he crossed the room preternaturally fast, sweeping Athena into an embrace. The goddess stiffened at first, shock widening her eyes. Awkwardly, she lifted her arms, returning her father's embrace with closed eyes.

An arm pulled me in as well. Who it belonged to, I couldn't say. I ended up sandwiched between Hermes's father and sister. Zeus's chest heaved as he sobbed. Athena's lip quivered as a tear slid down her cheek.

These were the last people I'd expect to feel for. I'd never been close to Carlo's family, so I hadn't expected anything like this from Hermes's godly relatives. Something about the tenderness broke down the titanium walls I'd built since Hermes collapsed on the floor of this very room, and I wept with my father and sister-in-law.

Eventually, we settled down among those seated.

Gabriel cleared his throat and with a sympathetic look in my direction, he said, "I'm sorry that Hermes was grievously injured. I am also—" The nephil-shifter paused, his gaze slanting to an orb that now hovered near his head. He grimaced at the device. Whatever he was going to say, we wouldn't hear it now. Or, at least not the whole of it. "What I would like to say is that I know what it is like to be unable to heal...because of a curse. I came close to death more than once that way. Miriam was able to help me because she is powerful and has a greater depth of knowledge than most. I have full faith she and the other healers will figure out how to help Hermes as well."

I forced myself to not glance at the camera orb. His admission of a weakness was gamble, but if he trusted his confession would garner what Hermes might need when all else failed, I had to as well.

A portal opened before us. A petite young woman with cropped brown hair wearing a black suit walked through. She still donned black lipstick and heavy eyeliner, but the twenty-something witch had an older air about her than the goth teen I'd known in Milagro Bay. I supposed Maria had seen a few things since she'd become an I.S.E.A agent. She nodded in my direction.

On the other side of the portal, Jada, with her curly green hair pulled into a bun, and also in a black I.S.E.A suit waited. Less serious than Maria, she grinned ruefully at Phyr, her adoptive father. I recognized something in his face. I likely had the same look of pride every time my Luke walked into a room. The fae prince returned his daughter's smile with a much warmer one than I've ever seen him flash.

"Agent Gonzalez." Maria flashed a badge and then furrowed her brow as she took in her surroundings. "I'm here to collect the specimen."

Rhiannon opened a door appearing out of nowhere, popping only her head inside the common room. "Wrong room, Jada!"

The green haired young woman frowned. "Agent Diaz when I'm working, Auntie Rhi."

"You can be gov scrub but I'm not calling you that, kid. Come on, you got to see this weird little sucker." Then the witch's big brown eyes cast an apologetic glance in my direction. "Sorry."

I waved my hand, dismissively. "No need. The worm *is* weird."

Jada walked through the portal she'd made and let it close, before following Maria through the Vault's door. Despite it being for tragic reasons, it was nice to see the adult kiddos among all this chaos. Their presence made me wonder what Luke was up to among the game makers. He had to know about Hermes. The two had created a bond of their own that had nothing to do with me. My chest ached and my eyes stung.

Not long after the girls left, Miriam came to the common room. The fae witch seemed tired in a way that we all were exhausted. "We're done. Now, we must wait until Inez and the forensics team have a look."

Bone tired, I rose to go back to my room. Miriam placed a hand on my arm. She smiled, bearing her fanged canines. From what I understood, she wasn't born with them and didn't realize how scary she looked when her sharp teeth made an appearance. Nevertheless,

I still had a case of the creeps, so I chose to focus on the concern in her eyes.

"It's safe to touch Hermes and talk to him. In fact, I encourage it."

Zeus joined me, his expression bleak. "I want to see him."

Although, all I wanted to do was to crawl into bed and sleep, I nodded. If it were Luke, I'd want to see him too. In the room, Zeus knelt by his son's bed. He appeared an older, grayer version of his son, but Hermes was lifeless or had the appearance of death.

Although I knew he was still alive but not, I shuddered. The state wasn't natural, and I couldn't let him stay a sleeping beauty forever.

Upon seeing Hermes's condition, the former king of the gods' face twisted with rage and grief anew. Zeus howled his rage. "He would never do this to another, not without provocation. He was my easy one, the most joyous and lighthearted god. All of us on Olympus with our politics and machinations needed his gregarious personality. He was a peacemaker among us. The messenger, the trickster, the guide of shades into a peaceful afterlife," Zeus buried his bearded face in his hands. "Hermes was not the warrior."

"I would like you to stop saying was. Hermes is not dead. We will find a way to fix this."

He lifted his face, eyes narrowed. "I had control over Olympus. I abdicated my throne. I live as a mortal farm laborer. I did all of it to avoid harm coming to my family, yet here we are in dire circumstances." He spread his arms. "Now, you want me to pretend that my son isn't going to die in a prison you placed us in."

"Yes. I do. Because he's not going to die, and I didn't place you in a prison. You volunteered to compete in games challenging for supernaturals, and so did Hermes."

Thunder rolled and storms brewed in the god's eyes. The odor of electricity filled the air.

He didn't scare me.

Not anymore.

The worst had happened, and he'd wept with me over Hermes.

He would not blame me for this and start a fight because he was angry and impotent to do anything about it.

Instead of cowering and apologizing, I nodded to the orb that followed us, got close to Zeus's ear as possible, and lowered my voice to a soft hiss. "And, if anyone watching sees that the king of the gods is weeping and gnashing his teeth, then they'll believe Hermes is a goner. My fiancé will *not* die because his father couldn't get his shit together."

Zeus backed away enough to take my measure. Whatever he saw in my expression stopped him from arguing further. In fact, the god pinched the bridge of his nose and said, "I'm sorry. Of course, we've volunteered to be here. I will focus on figuring out who has sabotaged our team. We're obviously considered a big enough threat to them that they tried to eliminate us by devious means. It might be more than one team conspiring against team Earth. I mean team red."

I might not have noticed if I didn't have sharp harpy eyes, but his gaze flicked to the orb more than once. The gods always played a longer game. I had to remember that.

TWENTY-FOUR

"Lydia, it is time to rise," the hologram announced in a cheerful tone.

My rest had been fitful and laden with nightmares, all about Hermes and worms, Apollo and Melinoë. Finally, I'd settled into dreamless sleep only for the voice to beckon me back to the waking world. I batted my way through the veil of sleep into wakefulness, grumbling about sunshine-y AI and wishing out loud for the flashing light in the cell I'd nicknamed Johnny. Still, I rose and got out of bed.

"You may call me Johnny. I liked it," the hologram replied with a wide, uncanny grin. It was close to human, but not quite and it triggered all sorts of alarms in my head that screamed *wrong!*

Already on my way to the bathroom, I froze mid step. "What did you say?"

"I remember when you named me Johnny. I think John is more suitable, but I don't mind."

I almost jumped out of my skin when the hologram blipped from one spot to right before me. She held out a hand and a small hologram of me lying on my bed in the cell appeared.

"Maybe I want to build some fingernail furniture or knit a hair sweater!" the miniature version of me cried out.

I cringed. "Not my best moment." The next thing I did was throw up my mental shields like a fortified wall over my mind. I'd thought she was part of a program I.S.E.A set in place. The fact that she was part of this former prison made my stomach knot.

"You're the same thing as the cell's...er...flashing words?"

"I am something much more advanced than the concept you're showing me," the hologram said, also revealing that my mental shields did squat against this whatever she was. She continued, "The interface was what Earth authorities called I.S.E.A. were capable of teaching me to do through basic language prompts. They've since had the help to bring me back to my full functions and give me upgrades. I didn't have the interface or language to respond then, but you were the only guest who spoke to me directly."

I was a prisoner, not a guest, but I was not going to remind the Vault of its former function.

She looked down at her hands. It was uncannily like a human displaying remorse. "I know they were imprisoned inside me. I didn't like it. I liked that you treated me as I am."

Swallowing hard, I asked, "What is that?"

The hologram smiled or at least did something like a smile. "I'm a sentient being. I think your people would call me a...god. Now, I have a name. It is John. This conversation is over. You must ready yourself for the Winner's Circle ceremony."

A short time later, showered and dressed, I paused by Hermes's bed. "Has there been any news from I.S.E.A's forensics team, John?"

The hologram appeared on the other side of his bed. "No."

"Do you know what that worm was and if it was keeping him alive or hindering his healing?"

The AI gestured to the door. "It's time for the Winner's Circle ceremony."

"John, do you know what is keeping Hermes from healing?"

John tilted her head to the side, her expression a facsimile of curiosity. "I do not understand the nature of your question. My function is to escort you to the winner's circle." The hologram was either was telling the truth or didn't want to answer the question.

I frowned. An orb hovered closer, capturing my reaction. With the near constant recording, the place felt less like games and more like 1984. At least the orbs weren't present when we woke up, in the bathroom, or when we were going to bed. The modicum of privacy had been appreciated. Now that I knew the very walls were sentient, which meant John had an angle of her own, I didn't feel the same.

JOHN LED me into the arena and through the teams of supernaturals gathered by their color designation. There were far fewer teams than the first gathering, which sent shivers down my spine.

Other versions of John led other winners, mostly my team, but there were others that my team hadn't faced yet who'd won.

The other members of my team had barely survived. Most barely survived the very first game and Hermes's life teetered in a limbo. Yet, I hadn't received so much as a scratch. It felt wrong and I couldn't help but wonder if John had something to do with it.

I doubted the Vault's projection as a hologram named John would admit she'd done something to make it easier on me than the rest.

As I walked to the stage among the winners, I didn't receive any congratulatory remarks. Instead, the other supernatural teams showered me with open glares, scowls, jeers, and threats. After years of lying low and not drawing too much attention, the open hatred set off all my internal alarms.

Gut churning, I kept my eyes on John as she led me to a stage with the other winners.

That's why I didn't see Apollo's approach.

"Who would have thought conwoman Francine Lawless would've competed against ancient beings of immense power and win?" His voice abraded like sandpaper in my eardrums. The question with the pause before "and win" for dramatic effect grated every exposed nerve.

However, I was still a woman who'd dealt with wise guys her whole life.

"I didn't know this was an audition for an eighty's movie bully antagonist, but you're doing a fantastic job, Apollo. Make sure you don't monologue though. That's where you cross over to spy movies and comics."

His grin flattened only a brief display of emotions before he covered it with a flash of brilliant white teeth. "Glib words and inconsequential references I don't understand won't change your fate. An Oracle should know that. Despite your disrespect, I still want you to serve me as one of the New Era Moirai."

"I warned you. You're now cast as a supervillain. Next, you'll take me to your evil lair. Bet it has bad guy groupies in sexy lingerie and gaudy gilded everything."

The god tilted his curly head back and let out a raucous laugh. "Oh, Lydia. Why not play the villain? You're playing the part of the hero, while everyone knows you're rigging games as if this were a two-stoplight town and no one can tell your crystal ball is just plastic—" He leaned in conspiratorially, making my skin crawl at his closeness. In a whisper only harpy ears could hear up close, he added, "Especially the people watching. You're really making this too easy for me by making it hard. I had to use all my skill and wit to win. I'm more powerful than I have ever been, thank you, Clotho."

I swallowed the lump in my throat and looked away. My eyes stung. *No, no, no.* I would not cry. He would not get that from me. It wasn't because I cared what he or anyone else thought of me. Thanks to Carlo I'd lost pride and dignity a long time ago—albeit I'd gained some since becoming Oracle. Not wanting to let Apollo see he'd gotten to me; I took the stairs onto the stage first.

Apollo followed close enough behind I could hear his snicker.

Rage crackled inside me like a live wire. This was all a game to him. A maneuver in an immortal's escape from boredom. He wanted to ascend because existence meant nothing to him. His own family were only steppingstones to godhood.

A dark thought occurred. There needed to be three Moirai. If I didn't make it through the games alive, let alone unscathed, Apollo wouldn't have his Clotho as he called me. Pulling myself out of that abyss, I realized something. Apollo didn't know or didn't care.

I turned to him but kept my pace. "Riddle me this, Joker. If I rigged the games, why is team red in danger of being disqualified?"

Apollo rolled his eyes. "What are you on about, Oracle?"

"One of my team members is dying. If he dies, I'm out."

He grabbed my arm. "Who?"

Tears welled in my eyes. "Someone who has done nothing but love you his whole life."

He sneered. "Zeus? My father didn't stop his wife from ostracizing my mother. He makes children then stands aside and enjoys Hera's jealousy. I had to prove myself to earn my place."

"Not Zeus," I spat, ripping my arm from his grasp. "See for yourself."

Apollo's gaze drifted over the teams, landing on the red team. Winners, most were making their way to the stage. The god's jaw dropped, and his eyes widened. "Where is Hermes? What happened to my brother?"

"Save it. If you cared about him, or any of your siblings at all, you wouldn't have ever started this." I turned away from the god, hurrying to the center stage to the winner's circle.

Spots of various team colors littered the stage floor, indicating where we should stand. The largest spot was red. Apollo joined Cronus, other Titans, Ares, and a few more Olympians that had won their games.

Thanatos, standing with Persephone and Hades, waved a bony hand in my direction, but it wasn't for me. Miriam drew close to me. She waved back.

As if just noticing me, Thanatos smiled and waved. Not that I could see his actual smile, but rather felt it radiating from some-where under his robe's hood.

Out the side of her mouth, Miriam asked, "So you two teamed up like Carmen and I?"

I smiled and waved at the God of Death. "Thanatos is a good buddy."

"Having allies is a good strategy but be careful. There may be many friends who turn enemies before the games are done. I think Hermes trusted the wrong person." She nodded at Apollo's team.

Apollo was in the middle of what seemed a heated argument with Ares. A good head taller, the god of war glared down at Apollo. Both turned in my direction. I held their gazes.

"You took a big risk, teaming with Carmen. Phyr said she has more motivation to kill you than help you," I said casually to Miriam as if my heart wasn't pounding in my ears. "Court politics."

"No, I didn't and no she wouldn't." Miriam sighed. "What Phyr doesn't know is that she doesn't want her children anywhere near faerie. She's playing games to make different courts think different things. Carmen is a survivor and in love with my father, not a faerie queen."

"You sound disappointed about that."

"I don't want to be heir. It would be better for me if my father's new love gave him a child and he transferred the role to them." She grimaced. "Unfortunately, Carmen will not be doing that."

I wanted to probe further, but I think she gave me a big secret shared in confidence about the wolf shifter. If there were more, she could say, the witchy fae would. "Speaking of which, your father was a contestant in my game,"

"Oh? Did he kill anyone and make it look like an accident?"

I blinked. "I don't think so."

The witch set her uncanny green gaze upon me. "Oberon didn't kill anyone to win and then made it look like an accident. Interesting."

Given I was his competition, I found her statement a relief rather than intriguing, but fae were fae. If only Hermes had allied with someone, maybe he wouldn't be hurt.

"He warned Thanatos that if he wanted to be your suitor, he would have to act accordingly."

"Ah, I see. He did try to kill his competition by proxy." Miriam smiled ruefully. "I'm glad my father only went that far."

Trumpets blared. We all turned to a holographic screen hovering between the stage and the arena below. One by one the screen played each victory. Then each winner was expected to give a small speech. They all seemed to know this and had something prepared— or at least, it sounded that way. I couldn't help but wonder why John hadn't prepped me. However, I didn't have long to contemplate what I'd say before it was my turn.

The spotlight shone on me, and I was speechless. *Come on, Lydia.* I had to make up a lot on the fly back when I was telling fortunes for a living. This was just an acceptance speech. After taking a deep breath with my eyes closed, I faced the drone.

"For the first time in my life, I am at a loss for words. Not because I am not grateful for my win, but because the games that I dreamt of were the sort of humanity has set as an example of goodwill. Yes, the competition has been fierce for the Olympics, but always without violence, without maliciousness.

I am deeply grieved that my fiancé, a god who has never harmed others, was mercilessly attacked to the point of near death. that others have died in these games..."

Shaking my head, I looked at my hands. I let the grief and worry of the night flow through me. Then, slowly, deliberately, I lifted my head, letting my tears, my grief, my *rage* show.

"I believe this is because I have lived most of my life as a mundane human believing gods to be flawless, or at least better versions of ourselves." I cut a glare in Apollo and his cronies' direction. "Why else would we worship them?"

I can't say that I didn't get deep satisfaction out of his throat bobbing or Ares looking away. Cronus, however, stared at me with an unreadable look. He seemed so far removed from the way his almost human Olympian children and grandchildren behaved, I doubted a public reprimand in front of believers would make him feel the least bit ashamed—or even scared. He'd survived without much belief at all and was still powerful. I decided I wouldn't put anymore thought into that titan. I didn't need their contrition. I needed those watching to think for themselves and maybe, just maybe allow those thoughts to shift their beliefs a bit. Perhaps even a lot.

"I am grateful for one thing. That is my teammates and for those who worked together in the games. Those who realized that there were no rules against two teams or more allying to achieve a common goal. Those who realized that winning might be the objective but weren't willing to compromise the lives of others to do so."

A lot of heads hung, but some glared. Those were the ones I noted to look out for. Those were the ones whose reputation as the good supernatural didn't matter. They wanted power and that was all.

"Thank you, Thanatos. Without your assistance, I wouldn't be here in the victor circle. Thank you, Miriam and the Baba Yaga witches. Without your quick medical intervention, Hermes's wounds from his ruthless saboteurs wouldn't be on the mend." I looked straight into the camera and did what I did for over twenty years, and I told the future I wanted my clients, and now my love, to have, "He should be fully recovered for the next game."

<h1 style="text-align:center">CHAPTER
TWENTY-FIVE</h1>

An hour had passed since I gave the speech and with each passing minute, Hermes's wounds healed, and his skin glowed a light magenta. He looked like a neon god. Color returned to his pallid cheeks and his features were more at ease. Miriam removed the stasis spell. We waited with bated breath for what would happen, but he took a deep breath...and still progressed. Whatever insidious agent had kept him from healing didn't stand a chance against billions of beings believing he would survive.

I should be happy. My impromptu plan had worked. Mostly. Hermes's eyes moved and his body twitched, but he still hadn't gained consciousness. I sat in a chair at the foot of the bed alongside the holograms of Agents Tan, Roanhorse, and Archimage O'Doyle. Orbs hovered, taking in Hermes's progress for the masses watching.

Here as an official I.S.E.A physician, Leilani, with her curly brown hair pulled back and dressed in her doctor's white lab coat and a stethoscope, examined Hermes. Her expression remained neutral and her hands glowed magenta as she waved them over the healing wounds. Finally, she turned to me and the waiting holograms. "He's in a healing state of sleep but should definitely fully recover by the next round."

Something in her deep brown eyes revealed she wasn't completely telling the truth, but I hoped that it was my former grifter ability to read people more thoroughly than average that allowed me to see the lie. Judging by the relieved looks in the agents' faces, I was correct to assume they didn't catch the look.

"However," the demigoddess doctor continued, "by the wounds and whatever agent was used to suppress his healing before, I'd deem this as attempted murder, which in my opinion, should disqualify the culprit."

The agents exchanged looks. It was Agent Tan who spoke, "We're waiting on the report from the forensics team. It seems the creature is not a wyrm or worm but might be an infant python."

"That thing didn't look like a common snake," Leilani replied.

"Not what we call a modern python, but rather, a descendent of the original being named Python,"

My brows scrunched. Python, a serpent-like dragon, had protected Oracles in the past. That is until Apollo killed the creature to take control of the then Oracle. It was the site where I'd called for these games. The circles of coincidence seemed too close. Even if he wasn't present in that competition, it would be sloppy work on Apollo's part. It didn't make sense after all that careful planning that he'd do something so traceable to him... unless it was the work of someone who was trying to frame him.

"At any rate," Tan continued, bringing me back to the moment. "Olympus has agreed to allow us to do testing on another python from that world to make sure."

I cringed. I didn't like the thing that had latched onto Hermes but, in my experience, what often looked like a monster to most was just a being trying to survive.

Tan glanced in my direction and with a rueful smile added, "Humanely test. The team just needs a blood and tissue sample.

Even the offending python will be released to Olympus after the test results confirm."

Nodding, I returned her smile with a closed lip one of my own.

"We're also going through every bit of footage and working with the Vault to see if it has any data about how the python got in. This won't go unpunished."

After the agents and doctor left, so did the hovering orbs. To my surprise, Tan's reappeared. "Nice save there, Kourakos. Way to play the system."

I looked at Hermes's sleeping form. His breathing was less labored and his face less still. "I had to."

Tan rounded the bed and faced me. "You did more than save your fiancé. The bloodbath wasn't what we'd expected, and we're looking into who caused it. I have an idea who started the trend and who put that python in place."

"Apollo?"

The agent shook her head, her black bobbed hair swaying with the movement. "I don't think it's him. We've had several unexpected events happen during these games."

"Who then?" I recalled Apollo trading angry words with the god of war. "Ares?"

She bit her lip as if stopping herself from saying too much. "Ares didn't put the minotaurs in the crevice game."

"So it's someone else from Olympus?"

"It seemed the cameras didn't capture how Hermes ended up with a python on him. It would be nice if we had a way of accessing a recording of that image we haven't seen so far." Agent Tan blinked a few times as if waiting for me to get some code.

I was used to reading people, but I had no idea what she was on about.

"Well, I have to go. I'll keep you posted on the lab results."

"John?"

The hologram of John appeared. "How may I be of assistance?"

"I would like to see the recording of Hermes getting injured."

The hologram tilted her head to the side. It wasn't quite the right angle for a questioning look, but she was close. "Why?"

Not expecting the question, I reared my head and threw up my hands. "Because I want to see it!"

John flinched. "Why are you angry with me?"

I clamped my mouth shut and closed my eyes, taking a deep breath. The Vault was ancient, but it seemed to have the emotional intelligence of a child. Which was incredibly dangerous. A child can't regulate their own emotions very well. John was much too powerful, a self-proclaimed god, for a tantrum or impulsive reactions.

"I'm not angry with you," I said, controlling my tone. "I'm frustrated because I don't know how the creature that bit Hermes got inside you."

"Oh...it was...a contestant! The contestants all thought Hermes was a threat, so they attacked him. There, you don't need to see what happened."

My stomach lurched. Luke was my boy scout, but even good little boys lied sometimes. Throwing all my mental defenses up, I thought long and hard about how to approach this. "John, were you sad when I left?"

"Yes. You talked to me. You talked to everyone, and everyone was happier with you here. Then Hermes came and took all my friends away. I was very lonely." John looked at her hands much the way I did when I was sad. She'd watched me for months and knew all my mannerisms. Her face brightened. "Then your genetic derivative and his friends taught me games. I knew more friends would come, and I wouldn't be alone anymore."

Oh, shit.

Did I have some sort of Hal situation going on? With Apollo's machinations, other contestants, namely Melinoë, wanting to kill me and make it look like an accident, and the challenges themselves, the last thing I needed was the Vault to become dangerous.

"John, were you alone before the angels found you?"

"Yes. For longer than is conceivable to your brain. So, I agreed to be a place where they stored people. They left eventually, but the people stayed. They kept me company and I took care of them like I took care of you."

I smiled gently at John. "You made all my favorite foods."

"You left."

"I did. This isn't where I belong all the time. However, I can come back and visit you when the games are over. We could make the games a regular occurrence, you can meet new friends. Unfortunately, no one will want to do that if any more contestants die or get hurt by minotaurs or pythons or any unplanned contestants or influences."

John blinked and then seemed to consider my words. "You won't be able to come back if Apollo wins. He and Cronus want you to be a Fate so he can ascend, and Cronus can rule with control of the reading of the weave. No more prophecies, Oracle."

"If they gain enough belief, they will ascend and become unaware of anything they wanted before they were omnipotent and omniscient."

The hologram flashed bright white teeth. "The loophole."

"The loophole," I agreed, wondering which thought she snatched *that* concept from, and finally deciding it was best not to ask.

TWENTY-SIX

Hermes sat up and flexed his fingers. He'd gained consciousness shortly after John's hologram disappeared. Slowly but steadily, he gained control of his faculties. I helped him use the bathroom and hovered while he cleaned up.

"I thought I was dying." The dark slashes of his eyebrows scrunched together.

It didn't take long before I gave him an entire rundown of what happened after his collapse in the common room. Hermes listened, wrapping his arms around me. "My clever bride saved me."

Belief saved him, but it was a one trick pony. Any more near scrapes would be on us.

A grin touched his sensuous lips. The god looked good for someone who was near death not long ago. Instead of the usual butterflies, tears burned my eyes. Hermes wiped one that escaped down my cheek.

"We can't rely on that a second time."

"Your wits have gotten us thus far. I have faith that we shall triumph."

I wavered on telling him about John and her sentience. I hadn't told Tan, but she'd guessed, or at least I thought she did. Also, Hermes would be rightfully angry with the Vault for trying to kill him to make me stay—which I couldn't quite prove either, but I guessed. It would take the lab report to tell if the python was from Olympia or a fabrication like the food John had made by recreating images in our minds. I also didn't want to think about what the source material was. Taking communion was one thing, but knowing we were literally eating a god didn't sit well with me.

Call me picky.

"About that. How about we do just good enough?"

Hermes scowled. "What do you mean?"

"I'm not in this to power up, are you?"

He had the decency to lower his eyes and not lie. However, I didn't like his answer.

It was my turn to scowl. "Hermes did you antagonize the fight?"

"No! Well...I am fast. Faster than any of them. They know this, *and* I may have reminded them." He scratched the back of his head. "You know, for the drama viewers crave from reality TV."

I pinched the bridge of my nose. He was older, but sometimes the trickster god made me feel like I was the senior in this May December romance. "The games are hard enough. Don't start anything. Just breeze by and let everyone do their thing."

The god breeched the distance between us, cupping my cheeks. "I will not put myself in harm's way again."

He leaned in kissing me softly and I forgave him. How could I not? He was alive and this was our second chance to get this right.

After we had some time together, we joined the common room so everyone, including the cameras, could see that he was fine. Athena and Zeus came in, father and sister tearfully embracing Hermes. I found myself in a four-way hug and not at all mad about it.

The rest of the red team piled in, making the large room seem like a tiny space. We were all jubilant though. Hermes pulled through, and we were still in the competition. Hope sprung in my chest that the first game would be the last deadly one.

"Alright. There's something that needs to be said," I announced, after everyone settled back into their seats. "We have to let the Olympians win. In fact, we need to ensure it."

A hush fell over the room.

"This is only a distraction. To stop the war, we need to take them out without killing them. The best way to do that is to let them win. Not only that, but we also need to convince the other teams to do so, as well."

Gabriel stroked his chin. "I don't know. What if it's not enough for ascension and we make them almost impossible to defeat?"

"Can you return to the Moirai?" Athena asked. "They could show you his thread without him knowing."

My stomach dipped at the thought of going to the Fates. "I don't know. They called me before. I'm not sure my body was there, only my mind."

"It was not," Hermes assured.

"I can take you to them," Phyr offered. "I'll need—"

Hermes waved his hand, cutting him off. "No, the temple of the Moirai is a place not even I can access."

The fae prince gave the god a lazy smile. "I am not you. You navigate the roads. I *make* them."

"Uh oh. Those sound like fighting words," Arachne quipped. Rhiannon was the only one to laugh.

The tension in the room thickened. I fully expected a pissing contest to follow, but Hermes nodded slowly. "No. This is true. I am a traveler, not a planeswalker, but this is a thing that has never been done. Lydia is the first known Oracle to have contact with them."

Phyr's grin widened. "I like a challenge."

Miriam rolled her eyes and exhaled a long-suffering sigh. "Anam cara, challenge and impossibility are two very different things."

"Yes. One is something I've done and well. The latter is a word that applies to others." The fae prince turned to me. "Do you have anything of the Fates that I may use?"

I shook my head.

He sat back and stroked his chin. Finally, he said, "The way I track someone down with an object is finding their light, which is their magical signature, if you will, of their past and their present, a trail through the multiverse we all leave. I cannot read the light that Lydia calls threads with my mind like an Oracle, but I can follow them."

"Is that how you gave me a way to find you with the mirror?" Miriam's face had a faraway expression, as if she were remembering something. "Was that a remnant of your light I was following?"

I didn't know what mirror she was talking about, so it had to be prior to my time on the supernatural council. Phyr seemed to know. He genuflected in his chair, which the fae made graceful somehow despite not getting up. "Precisely so. I simply used the mirror as a tracking device of my whereabouts."

Miriam looked pensive. "Huh. Interesting."

Interesting indeed. I rubbed my temples, trying to grasp it all.

Hermes leaned forward. "The way you follow these signatures or threads seems a lot like how I find those with the ichor of Olympus."

Phyr spread his hands. "I figured as much. Except, you follow the roads. I can make one."

Before the fae's smugness turned into a pissing contest again, I asked, "Do you think you can follow where I've been, even if it has only been with my mind?"

"Oh!" Miriam sat up. "They must've used a spell that allowed you to astral project into their plane. That's extraordinarily advanced magic. I would love to know how it works."

"The Moirai have been around since before Olympus existed." Athena scoffed. Chiming in on the conversation once more with, "Of course, it's *extraordinarily advanced magic*. The question is, would astral projection leave the same signature?"

Phyr stood. "There's only one way to find out."

TWENTY-SEVEN

The fae prince furrowed his brows in concentration as he manipulated the air around me. His usually amber eyes glowed bright green and his throat tattoos lit up. The fae's magic had a different texture than the magic of the Olympians or the witches for that matter—it felt like the cool of a dense forest, a briar of soft wild roses, and the prick of stinging nettles all at once. Before the games, I could see the color of magic, but I hadn't *felt* the difference. It all had a slight tingle. This new ability worried me. Unfortunately, I couldn't vent my fears to those close to me, not now with everything else at stake.

Phyr's glowing eyes widened with excitement that colored his voice. "Got it!"

With one hand above my head and the other waving before him, he made the air ripple like waves on a pond. Nothing more happened. He waved his hand again. Again, the air rippled. He grimaced.

John appeared. Her hair was slightly different than before. The texture had been straight and long, now she wore it curly, pink, and short. That wasn't the only difference. She was taller and willowier.

Her features had sharpened and her skin shimmered. She looked...
fae.

This wasn't my John but rather the one that must appear for
Phyr.

"No contestant may leave the premises during the games, or
their team forfeits the right to compete."

Phyr's face lost all expression. The feel of his magic slipped away.
Everything about him receded. It was as if he'd been a warm, shining
light and had dimmed. Miriam, too, seemed different. That eldritch
part of her that lurked just behind her eyes woke as if slumbering
until this morning. Others tensed. The whole room might as well
have shouted, "Danger, Will Robinson!" They had not assumed John
had been a simple hologram as I had. They knew exactly what she
was. How had I been so naive? I'd been around supernaturals. I'd
been imprisoned here. I could have kicked myself for thinking she
was an AI hologram. I was the only one who didn't get that the Vault
wasn't an *artificial* intelligence, but rather, a powerful magical entity.

While others saw her as a threat, I thought this was a good thing.
If John wasn't a programmed machine, then she could be reasoned
with, right?

"Johnny, I need to consult the fates. It won't give—"

The fae version of John gave me a fanged smile that made my
blood cool. "Knowing the future will give you an unfair advantage."

"I could read the future from here. It's my gift. Using our talents
is acceptable under the rules." I gestured to Phyr, who could have
been made of stone for all he moved. "He is only using his gift to help
me use mine."

The fae version of John lifted her chin. As she regarded me down
her nose, her eyes narrowed in the pompous way I'd seen Phyr, and
the others use when they were assessing someone. She lifted a
dubious eyebrow and asked in an imperious tone, "Is that so?"

The utter faeness of her mannerisms and speech sent a shiver
down my spine. She'd seemed so...well, innocent when we'd chatted
before. Johnny was learning. The question that burned in my mind

was for how long. A good portion of her "guests" had been prisoners from the war between the angels and fae.

"John, I am looking for an outcome but not to the games. I need to know if these games will bring about peace or war."

"Also, we need to determine if Lydia will be forced to serve as a Moirai for saving us all, " Athena added.

John turned her attention to Athena, then back to me. Some of the pretension slipped. Genuine worry filled her eyes. "If you don't leave, you won't. No one can force you. I won't allow it."

My mouth went dry. I was good arguing on the fly, thanks Carlo, but I never had this much pressure. "If I don't leave, there will be war. I promise I won't cheat. I know this is against the rules but as I've said, more is at stake than the games."

I didn't know if a being like John would care about people far away. I didn't know if she cared about me other than she liked that I'd named her.

She mulled over what I had to say, or at least made the appropriate expressions to convey she was considering my plea. It reminded me uncannily of the way Oberon looked as he coldly told Thanatos what he needed to do to win Miriam's heart. She didn't have human expressions down, but she certainly knew how to act like a fae noble. "If the games are successful and there is no war, will everyone return to me on a regular basis?"

Despite acting like a callous fae, John didn't want to be alone. That much was clear. I could work with that. However, the fae didn't lie. I would have to keep that in mind. To be fair, they were also masters of evasive speech. I'd have to keep that in mind, too. I swallowed hard, deciding to go with a truth. "That's how the Olympic games on Earth work. Most competitions do."

"I would like you to promise that you'll come back."

That was easy.

"I will come back."

Magic pricked my skin warm and tickling like a Mediterranean breeze and feather strokes all at once. It was my own magic binding me. Promises had bound me since I signed my name in blood, receiving my gifts, but when and *how* did my words become binding? I was not fae. I was, however, gaining strength. Was this some of the autonomy given up on the way to ascension?

"You may break the rules, but only this once." John grinned. "I will keep our little secret as long as you keep your promise."

With that, she disappeared. At least the image of her did. John was right here, under my feet, the walls, the ceilings, even in the air I breathed in my lungs. *That* made me claustrophobic enough that I welcomed Phyr trying and succeeding at opening a portal to the Moirai's Temple.

I walked through into the forest path I'd arrived on before, expecting the fae prince to follow. When he didn't join me, I turned around. Phyr and someone who looked like me stood on the other side. The look alike collapsed. Hermes, lightning quick as always, caught her. His face a mask of terror as he regarded the limp doppelgänger and then lifted his gaze to me. Even Phyr blinked. The others gathered around the fae, Hermes, and my look-alike.

"Lydia?" the god called, paling visibly. "I don't understand?"

Panic shot through me like a splash of cold water when I realized he was talking to the body and to me, because we were both me. I looked down at my hands, expecting them to be transparent like a ghost in a movie, but I was solid. Was I dead?

"You're astral projecting," Miriam said, clearing some of my confusion. "Let's talk later about how that happened without a spell!"

"How do I get back?"

"There should be a thread of your light between your spirit form and your corporeal form," Miriam replied. "Can you see it?"

I focused. There were so many threads making up the weave of the forest. It was difficult to spot one. A shimmering magenta strip light with gold sparks connected me to the woman in Hermes's arms. I sensed I could follow it back, alleviating some of my panic.

"I will keep the portal open, but I can't follow." Phyr pointed behind me. "It seems you were expected."

Rather than myself turning around, my perspective and place where I stood shifted. Before me, the three Moirai, Clotho, Lachesis, and Atropos waited. Gauzy veils covered their heads and their chitons moved with them as they sat upon stools. One spun. One measured and wove the thread into the forest skein. One unraveled individual threads from the forest and cut with a decisive snip.

"You promised him to replace us," Clotho said, shaking her head mournfully. "That was a mistake. You cannot keep it."

My heart lurched in my chest. "I didn't mean you harm. I only agreed, hoping to distract him as you told me to do."

Atropos snorted as she snipped another life away. "Do us harm. You cannot."

Okayyyy.

Clotho reached into somewhere unseen, pulling a glowing fiber to add to her spinning. "Do you understand what we are?"

Having no clue, I worried my lip. Then, based on what Apollo wanted from me, I made a guess. "You were once mortal women who became ascended gods?"

Atropos laughed, the sound was high and bright like tinkling bells, the way an adult laughs at an innocent toddler's naïveté. She then took another the length from the forest and cut it with a pair of silver shears. The light died first. The thread went limp and turned to ash. She brushed off the expired life from her hands like powder.

"We are and we are not," Lachesis explained, measuring a length of glowing string that Clotho unspooled before feeding it to a loom that wove the thread into the forest. "We have not ascended from a corporeal form. We have existed as we are in this realm for all of eternity and have gone by many names. Apollo believes us as flesh like him because he cannot fathom that we are what we are."

"He is so smart yet so stupid," Clotho agreed, spooling out more glowing thread to her sister. "He cannot kill us or replace us, even with the power he seeks."

I decided to be direct and ask what I wanted to know. "So, if he wins the games, will he start the war or will he ascend?"

The three Fates exchanged glances. Lachesis finally spoke, "You must continue to distract him. That is all. "

Anger boiled up. Hermes had almost died. My friends had suffered grievous wounds. We were pushed to our very limits and only one competition had passed. They knew the future, they'd spun the threads, measured, and cut. They had personally given me this mission. The least the Moirai could do was tell me that this wasn't all for naught. "You showed me a catastrophic war! I want to know if this distraction is working or for nothing!"

Atropos spread her hands, holding a thread and her shears apart. "It's unclear."

I couldn't help but watch the thread. Someone's life just hung there in the balance as she gestured. My mind spiraled, but I was a fighter. Closing off those thoughts, I drew on my outrage that I was in this predicament in the first place. I wanted to stomp my foot and scream, but I was a middle-aged empty nester, not a teenaged girl. I knew the only thing certain in life was that there was no certainty, no guarantees, but I'd wanted one. The Fates had their duty to maintain the threads of the whole tapestry, but ultimately, they didn't control the outcome. Still, I had to ask...

"Why?"

Clotho and Lachesis, still spinning and weaving, bowed their heads. Atropos glared. "Tell her."

Clotho finally spoke. "The fibers have multiplied. A myriad of threads that split in so many ways, no single yarn is clear."

"This is a rarity. In all of our existence, we have not seen so many possibilities." Lachesis waved her hand. "See for yourself!"

A door that hadn't existed before opened, revealing a chamber... no...not a chamber. The entrance was small, but behind the door lay an entirely different realm so vast that I couldn't perceive an end in any direction. "The Source was never a finite realm. However, it grew to accommodate the fibers that multiplied when your friends revealed the existence of the veiled peoples and realms to humans. It grew more when you announced the games. It continues to grow, and our work is too much to see it all anymore."

"Beliefs have changed, and belief is the very center of destiny," Clotho said.

"You could have just taken him and Hermes as lovers," Atropos shrugged. "That usually causes enough trouble with the Olympians to distract them for a while."

The sisters nodded and laughed.

I blinked. "Did you just make a joke?"

"Yes. The truth is funny." She dusted someone's life off her hands, picking another thread.

"What should I do?"

The sisters all regarded me with curious expressions, speaking in unison, "We are merely witnesses to it all. What you do has always been up to you."

Suddenly, I felt a jolt in the pit of my stomach. Like someone had tugged on a string. Everything went black, but I had the impression of moving a long distance at a rate faster than Hermes could run. My eyelids fluttered open, and I was in his arms.

"What did the Moirai say?" Gabriel asked.

I sighed and threw up my arms. "We're on our own."

CHAPTER
TWENTY-EIGHT

When the holographic screen appeared announcing our next game, I thought I'd be more wary. Hermes didn't seem reticent at all, either. We simply got up and got ready the way we'd get ready for any other regular day of training. That is, until we got to the door. Hermes pulled me to him in a tender embrace. The adoration in his eyes as his gaze swept over my features, married with the intensity of my reciprocal feelings, overwhelmed me. I'd thought I'd known love, but the teenage romance between Carlo and I fizzled out. We became coparents, partners, but not lovers. Maybe it had been intense, once. I couldn't remember. It had all faded over time.

Would this feeling last between us?

For now, I'd let that fear go. There was no time for second guessing. No space for contemplating whether we would last. Tomorrow wasn't promised and so we had to be present here and now.

He said nothing, at least not with words. Heat and tenderness swirled between us in a passionate, yet tender kiss. Reluctantly, we pulled apart.

"We will make it through this, and we will marry on a beautiful, sunny day," Hermes assured.

Uncertain, I could only smile in return. It seemed to be enough for him. As I watched my love go through the door first, I could only hope he was right.

~

I ENTERED A LONG YET narrow room. The ceiling was so far above and the end of the room so far away, I couldn't see either, not even with my harpy vision. The walls of the room were covered in moss. The ground below my feet consisted of the same sort of spongy texture as moss but possessed a deep purple hue.

The contestants all seemed to be there already. I guess the kiss lasted longer than I thought. Someone familiar waved. Lucinda made her way to me. Her dark curls were tamed in a top knot. She wore her team's colors. Next to her, another familiar face filled me with delight to see. Cosmo's hair and beard were neatly plated. He had legs for this competition. His muscles bulged in the T-shirt and track pants as he ate the distance between us. He picked up his pace, scooping me off the floor and lifting me up as if I weighed nothing.

"Lydia! It is so good to see you!" Cosmo's booming voice echoed back from the walls.

Other competitors turned to stare. I didn't care about their reaction, but I did have a problem with not being able to breathe. The general of the seaman navy's hold evacuated all the air from my lungs.

"Cosmo, she's turning blue." Lucinda's tone reminded me of a mother correcting her children, not one general speaking to the other.

"Apologies!" The big seaman loosened his hold, allowing me to slip to the ground, and more importantly, breathe.

I waved a hand, forgiving him and dismissing the notion he

needed to be forgiven at once. Breath caught, I said, "Thank you for helping Nora out."

Cosmo's cheeks flushed. "I-I...How is she?"

I grinned. "Good, my friend."

He shared my smile. "She's the bravest human I've ever met."

"So," Lucinda interrupted. "Hermes recovered?"

Grateful she asked, I nodded and turned my grin in her direction. "Fully recovered." With less enthusiasm, I added, "He's competing today."

With concern in his eyes, Cosmo squeezed my shoulder with his large, comforting hand. "He will make it."

"So will Nora," I teased to watch his face turn bright crimson. I wasn't actually sure how well she'd do. The mundane had a boost from Athena and had gained power of belief. What that meant against beings powerful enough to take down a god remained to be seen.

He stammered a bit for finally managing to say, "Of course."

Lucinda's eyes narrowed at the same time as someone tapped my shoulder. Behind me stood Carmen. Her dark hair was pulled back in a sleek ponytail. She wore the green of the fae, but there was nothing fae about the shifter. Oberon's consort and royal pain in poor Miriam and Princess's asses. The shifter gave me a wolfish smile. "Fancy both of us here again. Don't worry. Oberon wishes me to not side with Olympus—although I think they'll win. My king doesn't suffer anyone who opposes his heir or her allies."

"One would think you'd be loyal to Miriam for what she did for you and your family," Lucinda chastised.

A low growl of warning that had no traces of human came from Carmen. "She let me rot here and took my children because I hit on her man."

Lucinda wagged her finger. "That's not the way of it, and you know it."

Carmen dropped the wolfy-tone and asked in her sultry, human voice, "Do I? Hmm...Miriam had the power to wipe out the whole planet, command legions to do her will as easily as a puppeteer pulls the strings of a marionette, but she plays by mundane rules. Where is her loyalty to her own kind? She's not even here as a representative of the Unseelie Court."

The siren general shook her head. "Miriam is loyal. If you had an ounce of leadership skills in that skull of yours, you'd know that avoiding war by making alliances and compromises is the way of true rulers. If she had used brute force, other supernaturals would have opposed and stopped her. The consequences of her actions would've rippled into the fae world. They are not ready for another war."

"Most aren't ready for war. Isn't that why we're here?" An arrogant voice boomed behind me. Almost seven feet of muscle and armor, Ares made an imposing figure. He had a slight resemblance to Hermes and Apollo, favoring his father's looks over Hera's beauty.

Lucinda and Cosmo stiffened, but Carmen eyed the God of War as if he were a raw steak. For all her talk of loyalty, it wasn't clear if she wanted to devour him...or rip off his armor and devour him in a completely different way. Perhaps that was on purpose. He was at once a threat and handsome.

However, I had no mixed feelings about Ares. He took part in a sabotage on his own brother. He may have even planted the damned python on Hermes.

He addressed Lucinda, but his gaze was completely fixed on me. After taking my measure, the God of War tilted his head to the side, curious. "What did you hope to accomplish with these games? You cannot avoid the inevitable. The multi-verse has had its cycle of peace. My aspect must have a season or there will be imbalance."

For once in my life, I was speechless. I hadn't expected Ares to be articulate, let alone express that war was part of some natural cycle.

I shook my head slowly. "War is not necessary. Conflict resolution doesn't need to resort to violence."

"Oh?" He arched a dark eyebrow. "Did you resolve your differences with Scylla, or Amphitrite and Charybdis, peacefully? I must have heard lies about you. For I heard you raised the sword of your forefather Perseus against them."

I swallowed hard but didn't waver from meeting his gaze. I hadn't even tried to talk to Amphitrite, Thetis, nor any of the undead naiads to get them to stop. *No.* I wouldn't let War get into my head. I had no choice but to fight. I lifted my chin. "That was beyond resolution, I defended myself and my home from attack."

A smug grin touched his lips and pride sparked his eyes. *Ares was proud of me?* "I know, and it was spectacular to behold."

No, he wasn't proud of me. He was proud that he made me admit that war was necessary when you had to defend yourself. Instead of letting him bait me further, I tried another tack. "I was in my rights to defend. You tried to kill your own brother unprovoked."

His pride vanished, replaced by a bored look and a shrug. "We fought. He lost."

I wouldn't let it go that easily. "Did you plant the Python on him to make sure he wouldn't heal?"

Ares's whole face darkened. "No."

Noticing I hit a nerve, I pushed, "Why not finish him off? Less competition for you."

Anger twisted his features into a mask of rage. His nostrils flared. However, the god didn't act. Didn't speak. He simply boiled in front of me. When he finally spoke, his tone was soft, but still limned with indignation at the accusation. "Careful, Oracle. I have loved Hermes much longer than you have even existed."

I didn't think Ares was lying. He truly thought he'd only slowed Hermes down, not almost killed his brother...and he felt guilty about it. This family feud made no sense to me. At the moment, I didn't care why they fought if there was still love there—I only wanted answers to what happened to my love. "If you love him, who did it then? Who brought a Python from Olympus? They should be punished for almost killing Hermes."

The God of War breached the space between us, whispering in my ear. "Pythons are extinct. There was *one* minotaur. "Ask your game makers of I.S.E.A what they gain from all of us dying in battle here, rather than warring on their world.

My jaw dropped. I'd figured John or Apollo were behind all the trouble. Ares backed up, smirking, hooked a finger under my chin, closed my jaw, and walked away.

TWENTY-NINE

Above us, Agents Tan, Roanhorse, and Doyle appeared in black suits and a robe, respectively. As before, Tan spoke for the trio. "Due to the violence in the last competition and the disregard of fair play and safety of fellow competitors, we had many requests to cancel the Mythic Games and were almost banned from showing the competition on many worlds. However, the judges had a meeting about it and decided that we will give every team a chance to redeem themselves, not only to those who played fairly but to those watching at home. However, the rules have changed."

She looked to Roanhorse, who took over speaking. "Only the contestants who rank in the top ten in this round will make it through to the next games. If no one on your team makes it into the top ten of their competition, the team will be disqualified from continuing in the games and will be sent home. Anyone who actively seeks to harm their fellow competitors will disqualify their team and will be sent home."

"You must win by your strengths, not by eliminating the competition," Doyle added for extra emphasis.

Cosmo leaned in. "Good to know with Ares around."

I nodded but didn't comment. I couldn't. My gut was roiling, and Ares had gotten into my head. Would I.S.E.A have changed the rules if viewers at home didn't demand the stop to the violence? I would not forget that the I.S.E.A allowed the bloodbaths by not stopping them.

"This competition will be a javelin throw." Tan did her best impression of a stern schoolmarm, crossing her arms and lowering her brow. "No javelins may be used as weapons against your fellow competitors."

"She should have left the warning to Roanhorse," Lucinda murmured.

Cosmo and I snickered. I put a hand over my mouth, whispering, "Tan does not play a bad cop well."

The ground trembling beneath us cut our mirth short. The floor slid away several meters ahead of where the contestants gathered. A platform covered with a massive pile of javelins raised from the depths. Instead of dogpiling onto the platform in a frenzy to grab a javelin, the supernaturals queued up. A few contestants started doling out javelins by the color of the shaft. The process didn't take long, and I was soon at the front of the line, reaching for the red one.

Before I could grab it, the javelin hopped into my hand. I yelped and gaped. No one else's javelin had done that.

Carmen clapped her hands and laughed. "Neat trick! Show me how you did it!"

I spared her a grimace but didn't comment.

"New ability?" Lucinda asked in Greek, using a hushed tone.

Having no idea what happened, I shrugged. "I guess."

"Hey!" Carmen protested, grabbing a green javelin. "No speaking in languages I don't understand. I'm your ally. You need to keep me in the loop."

"Telekinesis is rare." Cosmo grabbed his javelin. His face grim, he nodded his head toward those still waiting. "Let's keep moving."

Once everyone had a javelin, the raised platform lowered,

leveling out at the surface and leaving no trace of where the platform had been. A long strip of blue replaced part of the purple floor. More strips of various colors appeared in a line like rainbow piano keys. We'd been trained enough by the colored spots in the arena to assume that is where the game makers wanted us to go.

Fortunately, I ended up with Lucinda and Carmen positioned between me and Ares, the latter standing closest to the god. I didn't think he'd use the javelin against me, but a murderous wolf shifter with a proclivity for powerful and attractive supernaturals, and a siren general with a voice that could make even a Titan powerless, were pretty good buffers.

"Do we begin?" Cosmo asked no one in particular.

As if to answer, the word GO in English flashed before me. With no time to answer, I walked backward as far as the length of color would allow. Posing the javelin in the air, I sprinted. Once I gained good momentum, I pushed all the power I could into the throw. Electricity crackled along the length of the javelin, delineating it from the myriad of others in the air.

Some of the javelins clashed, landing in the near distance. The rest sailed for what seemed like hours but certainly lasted for a teeny fraction of a minute.

TENTH PLACE: TEAM BLACK

I whooped and hugged Lucinda in congratulations. Happy that she'd made it to the next round. Her skin glowed with her magic. It smelled of brine, and I could almost hear the ebb and flow of the tide and the call of seagulls in the distance. We disentangled for the next announcement.

Ninth, eighth and seventh places passed. Sixth place went to Carmen. She howled and so did her magic of deserts and mesas, evergreen forests, wild rivers running through valleys, fur and fangs. Pack and loyalty ran strong in the current of her power. There was an underlying glimmer of sadness. Carmen longed for the wilds of Earth and her people. In that longing, I could see tangles of machinations. I shivered. She wouldn't walk away from these games merely a wolf shifter and she knew it. She wanted her children and she wanted back on her world in a position of power. Belatedly, I offered her congratulations.

Fifth place went to Cosmo. His magic smelled and felt like Lucinda's. There were also images of the deep sea and coral reefs, massive whales and other creatures I'd only thought of as myths. He smiled softly. His eyes shimmered. "You'll place."

I hoped I would but placing this high wasn't the plan. Stay in the games, yes, but not at the top. I already experienced the changes one win brought me. It was overwhelming and I could feel a piece of who I'd always been dying with it. Was this what it meant to become truly powerful? Losing myself never was part of the bargain.

Lost in thought, I missed who won fourth place, the magic felt foreign and unrelated to Earth at all, but by third I was focused again.

THIRD PLACE: TEAM GOLD

A singular angel stood under a massive beam of sparkling light, their wings spread, and their arms lifted toward the light. The magic swirled, speaking of an airy place of sky islands and elegance.

SECOND PLACE: TEAM YELLOW

My heart lurched. I wasn't going to make the cut. Still, I'd be able to watch the games from the team room. Others had made it. I was sure of that.

Meanwhile, Ares pumped his fist in the air. The magenta aura about the mighty god was as bright as a spotlight. Neither his magic, nor the power he gained, was subtle. The roar of battle filled my ears. Mighty soldiers marched in my head. Ghosts of the fallen lay everywhere. A weary but victorious leader plunged his flag into the ground, claiming land that would keep the bellies of the widows and orphaned children full and bring him riches. Victory at the great cost.

It was Ares. A young Ares in Olympus the world, not the palace. His eyes met mine. He seemed to understand what I saw. The memory that filled his mind. Or, perhaps I'd gained the power to read the thread.

I'd learned a truth about Olympus. I'd only seen the palace. The world was disappearing. Only a fraction of Olympus was left. This was why Ares had sided with his brother Apollo. Why he was here. He felt Zeus had cowered too long from the angels. The god of war wanted his world to prosper again.

Was that why Zeus gave up Olympus so easily and let Apollo have it? He'd certainly gained power and likability with the games. Maybe getting Apollo out of the way to save Earth wasn't the thing I needed to do. Maybe it was time for all of Olympus to get an overhaul. My gaze swept over the contestants. Maybe all the worlds needed this as much as Olympus. What had the angels done in coveting belief? Yet, their religion wasn't what it once was. Plenty of people no longer subscribed. Was Heaven flailing to stay relevant without their deity at the reins? Their god was an ascended. The angels were as immortal as gods, but they were still flesh. They could be killed.

My swirling thoughts were swept under a storm of magic. It poured over and into my flesh, sinking in deep to the marrow, to the very center of my being. The place that could leave my body and walk among concepts to read the threads of people's lives. I could almost see the skein, the weave of it overlaying the game. My harpy strengths came next. My sense sharpened. Lydia Kourakos seemed a distant memory. I felt light and floating. I was losing my humanity... my body.

No!

The scream echoed from a distance.

"Are you alright?" Lucinda asked. Her hands were on my shoulders, her grip iron hard and talons out and digging into the muscle. "Stay with us. Don't let go," the siren whispered in Greek. "We need you, Lydia."

I concentrated on the pain; the warm, wet blood sliding down my arm. Thinking of Hermes, Luke, all my friends, and my life in Milagro Bay, I pulled myself back in.

"I'm still here."

CHAPTER
THIRTY

I breathed in slowly through my nostrils, holding the air in my lungs for a few seconds and then allowing the tension in my body to release as I exhaled through pursed lips. I'd gone through seven rounds. Team red had made it through seven games. I won all seven. I couldn't say the same for all of my team. They'd followed through with the plan, losing or barely coming in last. Sometimes I did everything in my power that wasn't absolutely obvious to not win, but it was obvious—to me at least—that John and perhaps those watching, weren't going to let me lose. Winning meant losing.

The final contestants were teams Gold, Black, Red, Yellow, Orange, and Green. Heaven, the Underworld, Earth, Olympus, Asgard, and the Unseelie Faerie. It didn't go unnoticed that there were many new believers in these old religions and that played a part. Asgard didn't have any representation on the Supernatural council. Perhaps after this, we should ask them.

For Earth I had Hermes, Athena, Arachne, and Nicky with me. The rest of the team lasted a couple more rounds but seemed to always have the odds stacked against them and in favor of my four closest friends and family. We all suspected John had a hand it in, but it might be I.S.E.A's doing. It might have been Luke. We wouldn't ever know. Perhaps it was because the rest of the council were lesser known over a long span of time, but that wouldn't explain why Nicky and I were here.

No, I was certain John wanted me to have those who I relied on most at my side, and I wasn't mad about that. Neither was the council—-Gabriel got over himself, and the others on the council, shifters, and the witches were relieved to no longer have to take part. For Heaven's team, there were four angels I didn't know at all, but the full angel Gabriel I'd heard of. He was the nephil-shifter's father, and a giant, arrogant jerk. At least he'd helped with the rescue mission and agreed to this competition. He gave me a cool nod. I didn't miss the way he looked at us, surprised his son wasn't among the winners. Interesting.

Melinoë, Hades, Persephone, Lucinda, and Thanatos had made it to the final round for the Underworld. All nodded or waved to us as they found the black spot, except Melinoë. The goddess gave me a gentle smile. Lucinda had said she'd gained more control over her wraith side. No wonder her parents chose her for the games. The power she'd gained helped with holding all the pain of so many people, I was sure.

She made her way over to us. Her mismatched gaze landed on Hermes. "I'm sorry." To us both, she said, "I hope your wedding is beautiful and you have a happy life together."

"You two still aren't married?" Carmen's voice came from somewhere out of sight, holding a tone of mild amusement. "Longest wedding preparation I've ever heard of."

To my left, Carmen, Oberon, and three fae who I didn't remember the names of watched from a green circle. Carmen winked at Hermes. Oberon grinned in our direction and whispered something in her ear. The look the couple exchanged said the high king of the fae wasn't jealous. The wink he gave the god confirmed Oberon shared his consort's opinion.

My fiancé certainly made my pulse race when I looked at him. However, I didn't like all four of the fae joining Carmen in ogling him. I casually placed myself between them and Hermes, smiled, and waved. "Stop teasing, or you won't be invited."

Carmen laughed. Instead of taking offense, Oberon gave me a once over. The fae king might be gorgeous, however, his flirtatious grin revealed sharp fangs.

I shuddered inwardly and subconsciously took a step back into Hermes's arms.

"She will be trouble," Melinoë whispered in Greek. "She is plagued by harsh memories and fierce loneliness. Her need to fit in with her new pack will make her even more ruthless than what got her here." With that, the goddess of nightmares returned to her place among the Underworld.

Instead of feeling afraid, I felt empathy for Carmen. The woman played at flirtation, but she didn't really want Hermes. Miriam had spilled her entire story. She'd fallen for the wrong man, too. Now, she was finding her place among the fae.

I turned my thoughts away from the other team and to my own. These four, strangers to me only a few years ago, were now integral to my life and as much family to me as Luke. I held the hope that John would grant them the same protection as she'd given me over the last rounds.

"We don't need to win," I whispered in Greek, nervous the statement would put the odds or the watchers in my favor. "We need to look like we tried and ensure Apollo wins. An ascended god won't start a war." I didn't add that I was barely keeping hold of my physical form.

Hermes nodded, squeezing my hand. "That's right."

Nicky also gave me an affirming nod.

"We know the plan," Athena replied tersely from my other side. "Perhaps you don't share it out loud with everyone else?"

I rubbed my forehead. "Sorry."

Arachne skittered around the goddess, wedged her round spider half in between us, and hip checked Athena aside. Athena sputtered in indignation. Arachne ignored her and patted me on the shoulder. "Don't listen to her. She's grumpy because she wanted Nora to be in this competition. Her prodigy was doing so well but that last round was a doozy."

"First you assault me, but you will not speak about me as if I'm not here." Athena sniffed, crossing her arms.

Arachne arched an eyebrow over her cat-eye framed glasses.

Athena's arms dropped and her shoulders slumped fractionally —a rare display of defeat for the goddess. "Nora has gained power at great costs. I only want to see her have as much magic as her indomitable spirit should have. Nevertheless, there are eyes and ears everywhere here. Err on the side of caution."

Holograms of Agents Tan, Roanhorse, and Doyle appeared on the stage. Tan stepped forward, her black shoes clicking against some far away floor. "For today's round, you will navigate a labyrinth. There is no object of power to find, however the winning team must be the first to find the center of the labyrinth after navigating the challenges presented. Good luck to you all."

The holograms of the I.S.E.A. agents flickered out. Portals opened before each team. I looked to my teammates, the people who had become my family and the best friends I'd ever had, and then I stepped through with them at my side.

The walls of the corridor we entered were made of white marble, a little yellowed as if time had weathered them. The stone had a feel reminiscent of Apollo's temple ruins, not the modern temple in the Washington Olympics. Like a Grecian urn or temple, murals etched into the marble depicted the rounds that occurred before this final round.

I cringed at the depiction of when I'd electrocuted Artemis. The horror on the goddess's face as if someone dear had betrayed her made no sense though. We were strangers. Weren't we? My mother's words echoed in my head about gods having complicated parts and that some were not as they seemed. Something else occurred to me.

Artemis could've wounded me and taken the object of power before I realized she was there. Instead, she threatened and demanded, but left me unharmed. Why? I had a sneaking suspicion and only Artemis could answer the question. The more important thing was, did I want to know?

An old wound that I'd thought had closed opened in my chest. The wound I'd always associated with my birth parents. I didn't want to think about it.

Catching sight of the orbs hovering overhead, I cursed. Damn it. They'd caught a weak moment. I wasn't sure if contrite was the angle I wanted to play, since it was Apollo I wanted people to sympathize with, and therefore root for and eventually gain belief, but it was too late. Magic sprinkled my skin, warm and soft like summer rain. I felt the strength of the power of those who rooted for me. If I were a narcissist or simply someone with a small ego, the feeling would be addictive. It only worried me because it was adding to what already made me feel like I was losing touch with who I was and becoming something else.

I swallowed that worry down.

Artemis's spider feet clicked on the marble floor under her red muumuu as she scurried back and forth, sniffing the air. "Anyone got a clue which way?"

"The progression of the mural events lead in that direction," Athena observed with a tilt of her head to the right.

Dipping into my harpy vision, I looked to the left and right and spotted a thin thread of golden light. I pointed to the left. "This way."

Athena squinted her eyes, facing the direction I pointed. "What is your reasoning, Oracle?"

Good. Good. Remind viewers of our titles. She was Athena, Goddess of Wisdom, after all. A little less belief in my strategy would turn attention to other contestants, namely Apollo, who would likely use the route she'd suggested.

"She can see the future, remember?" Arachne said, winking behind her cat-eye glasses.

Athena's mouth flattened and her tone turned dry as dust. "Oh, that's correct. The Oracle, whom I addressed as such, sees the future. Thank you for clarifying."

Arachne patted her on her muscular back with a frail hand. "No problem, sweetie."

Hermes chuckled.

Nicky placed her hands on her hips. "I wonder if the other teams waste precious time being smart asses or if they have actually started going through the labyrinth."

"They might have," I replied, grinning.

"But I bet they're not as fun as us," Hermes added.

All four of us started off at a light jog. Athena took a faster pace. Arachne scurried faster to catch up to her. I was worried that if I kept their pace, I'd lose stamina. I'd came a long way since the time when I sat around and told fortunes all day, but I wasn't born as fast as a goddess or spider lady.

Nicky glanced at me. "Do you think there will be a barrier against flying?"

"It wouldn't hurt to get an aerial view." I shrugged off my hoodie, the tank underneath was cut low enough for me to release my wings. Pain seared between my shoulder blades as bone and feathers tore from my back. I'd gotten used to it, but it hurt. Every. Single. Time.

I picked up speed, running as fast as my legs would push, and took flight. Nicky joined me in the air.

"We're going to scout a bit," I shouted to Athena, Hermes, and Arachne, who'd gained significant headway from where we'd started. Hermes was at the lead.

Arachne raised a frail arm and gave me a thumbs up. Keeping her pace, Athena only glanced over her shoulder to nod.

Nicky and I rose higher and higher. The sound of our wingbeats echoed back at us from below. Above, the sky was a similar sparkling firmament I'd seen in parts of the Underworld. We weren't hindered in flight by some invisible forcefield. The walls, however, seemed to stretch taller than I'd perceived from below.

I flew closer to Nicky. "Is it just me or are the walls growing?"

Her birdlike features pinched in consternation as she replied, "I'd hoped it was just me."

I didn't want to cheat but I certainly wanted to see where Apollo was at in the race. "Well, since we can't scout ahead, I guess we'll have to hoof it the old-fashioned way."

CHAPTER
THIRTY-ONE

To my surprise, the first part of the labyrinth was pretty boring. If we didn't look at the murals there would be nothing to look at. No twists or turns or openings. Simply what seemed like miles of corridor with no ending in sight. I thought there would be more challenges by now, like minotaur stampedes or some great monster to fight.

I didn't understand why I.S.E.A set this up this way. How would nothing happening make for good viewing?

The murals depicted a lot more than events in the arena. It was like watching a cartoon panel format of the longest home movie highlights of our lives for the past few years.

"All of these depict things that happened since I became Oracle," I remarked to break the bored silence. "There's nothing from my mundane days."

Hermes lifted his gaze to the wall where it depicted him having my back against Charybdis. He smiled. "I like that it is since we were formally introduced. Some moments I'm prouder of myself than others."

"Formally introduced?" I laughed. "You watched me jump building to building then mocked me for falling on my face."

He shrugged. "It was very high but a little jump, like a crack in the sidewalk."

"I fell down that crack!"

His responding grin and the way it made his dark eyes crinkle in the corners made my heart flutter. "And I caught you."

Athena glanced back. "That was not my proudest moment. I wanted to come to your aid, but I felt that obeying father mattered most."

I cleared my throat. Now was the time to introduce a theory that had been brewing in my head since the javelin competition. "Do you think that Apollo hasn't been doing this out of pure vanity?"

All four gave me a sharp look, only Hermes, who still loved his brother, gave me a curious look. "What else would be his motive?"

"He's the God of Music and Arts, and the Sun after Helios was locked away in Tartarus."

Athena furrowed her brow. "I fail to see your point, Lydia."

Oh, I was back to Lydia now? Great.

Lydia was her friend and soon to be sister-in-law. She acted like the French language, separating how one spoke formally to a position of authority and to their close friends and family. It was her subtle way of saying that she wasn't taking what I was saying as the official council as Oracle to a goddess, but instead as a discussion between family and up for debate. I'd learned this much about Athena since she'd come into my life. It was not a good sign for her official position, but a good sign for a sister who still loved her brother despite his actions.

"Well, he once carried Adonis across a field because he was so sorry that he'd injured him. He also seemed truly upset when he thought Ares had placed the python on Hermes."

"He killed Thetis and your own mother," Nicky countered. "He also almost killed Luke to get him to open Tartarus. Not to mention the harpies he slaughtered, and again, the war Athena mentioned."

As my late mother's life partner, I doubt she'd be able to see past that. As the child of one of those women, mother to Luke, and a harpy, I certainly had a hard time reconciling his purpose with those things, too. However, the memory of Ares justifying the carnage on the battlefield as a fair fight still weighed heavily on my mind. I didn't have to think the same way as someone to understand where they were coming from. That was the point where peace could be brokered.

"I'm not saying he's a standup guy on a personal level. Not at all. Have you ever heard of the term 'necessary evil'?"

Athena scowled but did not reply. Nicky scoffed. However, she also didn't argue, which was good. That meant she was against this theory but willing to listen. Hermes simply kept his gaze ahead, alert and listening. Out of all of them, I knew the siblings wanted a reason to not be their brother's enemy for eternity. If there was a way to reconcile this family feud, they'd be the ones to want to hear it out.

"There are those who believe that heinous acts can be done if it is in the interest of the greater good," Arachne answered. Her cheeks colored. She'd done some heinous things in the interest of protecting others, including something to someone precious to Athena.

I thought her reply had meant I'd had Arachne on my side.

However, she had not been on Olympus in a very long time, so she had more trouble suspending disbelief than the rest. "Explain how his megalomaniac machinations for a war that could destroy Earth and slaughter most of his family could possibly be for the greater good."

"Olympus is dying. The borders are shrinking, our sentient beings are decreasing in numbers, and many of the wildlife are going extinct," Athena admitted, her chin held high. "The prey first. The predators are becoming harder to manage and are also dying. Some of our flora, too."

Arachne skittered side to side ahead of us, she pointed to the battle scene outside Renee Charles, aka Leto's house in Medina. "Griffins and manticores?"

"Yes. I was surprised to find them on Earth for more than one reason. Griffins and manticore are rare to find on Olympus these days." I could hear the regret for killing the ones she had to in her tones. Her pride made her add, "It's true of all of the magical worlds that are sustained by belief."

She switched subjects before I could question her further. "You know, I don't think this was the correct course to take. It seems there's no end to this infernal corridor!"

"Not true!" Hermes pointed. "Look! There's an opening ahead."

I blinked. There certainly was an opening in the wall, however, there hadn't been one there a moment ago. It had depicted the battle and now it had a golden thread shining that the opening was the way to take instead of continuing down the corridor.

I gestured to the opening. "Is it me or did that opening just appear?"

"It's definitely not you," Nicky replied, face grim. Her eyes were on the orb floating above. "It's the right way."

Following her gaze, we all exchanged looks. The orbs were ever present, but in the games, the camera drones would fly closer when something big was about to happen. I could only hope it was because we were headed down the right path.

The opening lead to another hallway much like the one we'd been going down. Athena eyed the corridor with suspicion. "What if it is a false path?"

I shook my head. "It's not."

Nicky folded her arms across her chest. "Are you sure?"

"What's the worst that could happen," Hermes asked. "We have to double back?"

"The worst that could happen, dear brother, is that we are trapped inside The Vault for eternity," Athena griped, but there was no heat in it.

However, her words sent a chill slithering down my spine. John was lonely. What if we were all trapped here forever?

I shoved that disturbing thought aside and pushed forward. "I'm going this way. You can wait here or join me."

Joining immediately, Hermes, Nicky, and Arachne had my back.

Athena hesitated at the entrance. I couldn't blame her reticence. She was the Goddess of Wisdom. If she hadn't sussed out where I was going with my talk of Apollo's purpose already, she just might want to avoid further difficult conversation that would surely occur down this path. Or she might trust John and I.S.E.A even less than I did. Unfortunately, we had no choice in the matter either way. I'd rather move forward and try than perpetually remain immobile in indecision.

I kept going and didn't look back, as did the others. Albeit we moved at a much slower pace than we had previously kept.

As a last-ditch effort to keep us from going down the unknown, Athena called, "We can't separate!"

"Then join us," Arachne retorted over her thin shoulder, but didn't break her eight-legged stride.

It was several breaths before I heard the trod of Athena jogging to catch up. Hermes gave me a look that said he appreciated how I handled his sister. The truth was, I had no choice. None of us did. We had to play this game.

THIRTY-TWO

If I'd assumed that this corridor would be as uneventful as the last, which I hadn't, I would soon be disabused of the notion. Ahead, the tan stone floor transitioned to a dark green and yellow pattern for a long stretch before again resuming the pale color —or at least I *thought* it was a patterned section of flooring until I noticed that the floor wriggled and slithered.

My blood ran cold. The walls weren't the only place I'd face my recent past. Despite being accidental, Echidna's death still weighed heavily on me.

"Snakes!" Arachne declared my fear out loud.

Not just the presence of snakes, but also the scent of ozone mixed with petrichor—the odors of an oncoming storm, or rather, a Titan with a score to settle.

"Typhon is coming." I reached for Harpe, remembering too late that we weren't allowed weapons after Hermes's near death.

Hermes and Athena both glanced at me. The latter asked, "Are you sure he's here?"

I shrugged. "Maybe it's him or the labyrinth's version of him, but

I bet my home in Milagro Bay the snakes aren't the only thing we need to get past."

Nicky ruffled her wings. "Do you think we're allowed to fight someone who isn't part of the competition?"

I gave a rueful smile to the harpy who'd become a mother to me late in life. "If Typhon is here to seek revenge, I don't think we'll have a choice—at least I don't."

Athena cleared her throat. "I say we avoid the snake pit and go forward. Fight as a team against Typhon, and hopefully, get him to disappear again rather than face all of us at once."

We all agreed. Hermes and I released our wings. He grabbed Athena, and I meant to carry Arachne over the snakes, but the elderly monster shooed me away.

"I can cross past them just fine without wings."

To demonstrate, she scurried up the wall and across. The rest of us flew over the snakes. As I passed over. The pile shook, the snakes dispersing in every direction as Typhon emerged, then they slithered onto his form, becoming part of him.

I flew to the side, dodging a screaming animal head on his massive shoulders.

"Oracle!" the humanish head bellowed among the cacophony.

"Go ahead!" I shouted to Hermes.

Thankfully, he didn't argue. He couldn't fight with his sister in his arms. He flew himself and Athena out of harm's way. However, I didn't face Typhon alone. Nicky screeched a harpy cry. The sound was shrill but didn't affect me.

The same couldn't be said for Typhon. The Titan covered his humanoid ears with his grotesque hands. Unprotected, his animal heads yowled, barked, hissed, screeched, and moaned in pain.

"Get him, kids!" Arachne's bowling ball sized spider children burst from under her muumuu as she charged.

Snakes and spiders fought on Typhon's limbs and torso. Nicky and I screeched. The Titan grabbed one of Arachne's children, throwing the spider against a wall. It hit with a sickening thud, falling to the ground.

Arachne screamed, unhinging her jaw. Rows of razor-sharp teeth rotated within her giant maw. She jumped, latching onto one of his heads.

Athena and Hermes stood side by side, blasting a free space on Typhon's back with magic. Snakes withered and fell, but it had little effect on the Titan himself. He shot a bolt of lightning at the siblings. They dodged, but Athena wasn't as quick as Hermes. The bolt seared her side. The stench of burnt flesh hit my nostrils.

I sent my own lightning bolt in retaliation. Typhon easily captured the lightning and laughed, barked, meowed, and made all kinds of eerie renditions of laughter.

Orbs flew around, capturing the entire battle.

Typhon had been part of killing my mother, he'd assisted Echidna in kidnapping me, but he'd been trying to free his family. I'd killed his wife and child.

"Stop," I screamed in ancient Greek. "Everyone, stop! Truce!"

I had to scream it over and over until everyone relented. Typhon faced me. Even the Titan understood I wanted to speak.

"I'm sorry I killed your wife and your child, but I didn't want to fight them in the first place. I didn't want to kill them, but I was defending myself and will continue to defend myself and mine as long as you and yours attack us."

The monstrous creature listened, moving only to swat a camera drone away.

"Let's end this feud now. I promise I will no longer bring harm to you and yours, if you leave me and mine be. What do you say?"

Hermes, Athena, and Nicky watched from the sidelines. Arachne drew her children in and then made her way to the fallen one. She picked her spider child up and cradled the body in her arms. The way its legs curled, and the black ooze left on the ground made my heart sink, but I couldn't do anything for the spider or comfort my friend now.

His hideous central head made a face as Typhon considered my offer. Finally, with what would pass as a regretful look toward Arachne and her child in her arms, he said in heavily accented English, "Truce. Promise."

The magic of the truce bound us both. Typhon slid back into the floor as if he were made of nothing but light and shadow.

The stone wall trembled. A portion retracted like a sliding door, revealing another hallway. Despite seeing a golden thread, I didn't enter. Instead, I joined a weeping Arachne. Her spider child possessed no magical aura, which could mean only one thing.

I put a hand on my friend's thin shoulder. "I'm so sorry for your loss."

Arachne nodded. "Lex was only six hundred and seventy-two years old. A good boy. A brave boy."

"He will be missed," Athena agreed. Her own face was bone dry, but her voice quavered.

"Lex shall have a place in Elysium, among heroes," Hermes promised.

Arachne placed the carcass gently on the ground. The other spider children descended from her skirts. They circled their dead sibling.

"What are they doing?" I asked.

Arachne's watery brown eyes appraised me from behind cat-eye frame glasses. "You're not going to want to watch this. It's not how humans respect the dead, but it is for my kind. I'll catch up."

Taking her word for it, I hugged Arachne and headed toward the new opening—as did Hermes and Nicky. Athena stayed behind with her girlfriend. I shuddered at the sounds that followed as we passed into the next corridor.

THIRTY-THREE

A lifelong arachnophobe, I didn't think I'd cry over a dead spider, but I did. We all did. Lex wasn't as dear to me as Greg, but they were Arachne's children. I don't know if they were her actual children, and I regretted being too repulsed by spiders to ask. We either accepted the bits about our friends that weren't delightful or perfect, or we shouldn't be friends at all. I promised myself to get to know her children better and to stop thinking of them as pets.

Speaking of pets, I missed Cerberus. Having him on this journey would have made it easier. However, he didn't make it far in the elimination rounds. Now that Lex was gone, I was glad. I couldn't bear to lose Cerberus any more than I could lose anyone else I'd come to hold dear. The Underworld guardian had become an integral part of my family.

Not too far into the next corridor, we stopped. One reason was to wait for Arachne and Athena to catch up. After whatever gruesome ritual they'd performed, they would need time to regroup. Losing a child, whether Lex was her biological child or not, wasn't something one just endured.

The second reason is that the corridor ended at a beach.

As if we'd stepped out of the Vault and back to Earth, dark sand, a stretch of sea and bright blue sky awaited ahead. Red cliffs bordered the distance. I'd seen pictures of Greece my entire life and recognized this place, although it was a little different. This was a facsimile of a black sand beach on the island of Santorini. The vista didn't exactly replicate what I'd seen in the pictures of the island, only the red cliffs and the black sands. The ebb and flow of the lapping Mediterranean-like waves mesmerized as only the real sea could.

I couldn't help but marvel at it on another level though. What John could make and contain within her seemed limitless. She truly possessed the magic of a goddess. One more powerful than any I'd met.

I shuddered at the sudden realization, I.S.E.A were only playing at control here. John let them make the prison and the games, but she could change her mind at any time. Perhaps it was my stay that allowed her to let go of the prisoners. She'd seen something in me that allowed her defenses to be penetrated, to exist in solitude when she could have kept us all. I felt deeply honored in earning her favor.

There was a flip side to a being ingratiated with a being this powerful. Was she even bound to her promise to me? Here's to hoping John wasn't as capricious as some of the gods I'd met.

Nicky wrapped her arms around her chest, hugging herself. She spoke, dragging my thoughts. "We could fly over the sea to that island."

A golden thread glistened in a direction that wasn't toward the island. It led to open sea. The logical route would be to the island where we could rest. Anyone watching would know that I had an advantage that others didn't. Or would they?

"I don't see that in the weave as a way that leads us out." I pointed to the open sea. "That is the way we must journey."

"We don't know how long we'll be out to sea. Where will we rest?" Nicky challenged without directly saying I was full of crap, although her face and tone said she was thinking exactly that.

Ugh. This wasn't the time for her to call me out on my b.s. I wasn't guessing and wasn't completely fabricating—I did see *a* thread if not an entire skein—but I also couldn't talk about my advantage.

"There's a boat," Hermes pointed to what looked like a weathered fishing boat in the distance. "When Athena and Arachne arrive, they can take it and we'll take turns using the boat as a place to rest."

When Athena and Arachne arrived with red-rimmed eyes, the boat was agreed upon as the better choice since the island seemed barren. Athena rowed the boat with Arachne at the aft. Nicky, Hermes, and I took flight.

The thread led from the open sea to a narrow straight between two distant land masses. Something about this bothered me, but I couldn't place what. I scanned the shores, spotting nothing.

"I'm stuck," Athena shouted, her voice carrying over the wind.

Nicky pointed. "They are caught in a whirlpool."

Sure enough, the tiny boat carrying the goddess and monster were at the edge of a swirling vortex. I'd been too busy watching the shores to watch the actual water. The three of us dove down.

Hermes took the helm, and Nicky and I took the back, pulling upward to break the boat from the whirlpool and move it to smoother waters. Even with the three of us exerting all our strength, we couldn't lift the boat out of the water.

The swirling of the whirlpool intensified. Nicky and Hermes each grabbed one of Arachne's arms. Meanwhile, I hooked under Athena's armpits, lifting the goddess away in time before the water ripped the boat apart before swallowing it down.

The water below opened like a gaping maw. Correction. Not *like* a gaping maw, but an actual one. Rows and rows of shark teeth longer than I was tall turned inside the opening, threatening to slice and dice us like a food processor.

I flew up and back, struggling against an air current dragging at my wings and our bodies. The opening sucking in like a vacuum.

"Charybdis!" Athena shouted.

At the same time, Hermes bellowed, "Undead!"

He and Nicky had escaped Charybdis' mouth only to land on a shore filled with exactly that. On the previously empty shores, the undead naiads, melusine, and other supernatural creatures of the sea rushed the shores. Among them, Thetis stood. Her eyes blazed with vengeance.

My stomach lurched and my chest grew tight with dread as Hermes, Nicky, and Arachne faced yet another fight.

Not only because they were in danger, but I didn't want to fight Thetis again, not after knowing it was Apollo who killed her. We weren't on opposing sides. However, I didn't have time to negotiate. My hands were full, trying to keep myself and Athena from getting eaten by Charybdis. Weaponless and helpless with Athena in my arms, I screeched my harpy cry.

The monster seaworm careened away from the sound of my voice. The movement took us out of the path of the powerful vacuum of her maw. I flew away from Charybdis toward the shore.

"Drop me!" Athena demanded.

She didn't have to ask me twice. I released her and the burden of her weight. Muscle-bound goddesses weighed a ton. She dropped to the ground landing in a crouched stance. The battle on shore began in earnest.

I swooped down and plucked Thetis from the melee. She was lighter than Athena but fought to be free. She clawed at my arms around her waist and snapped her teeth just missing my face. Her nails dug into my flesh. The searing pain called to an instinct to fight back or at the very least to drop her ass in Charybdis' mouth.

Instead of caving to that instinct, I cried, "I'm sorry!"

I said it over, over, and over again. Tears streamed down my face as I sobbed the words. I truly meant it. I was sorry that Zeus and Poseidon used her for her body when she was clearly so much more than that. I was sorry that Apollo also used and betrayed her. I was sorry that we were enemies when I had nothing against her. I was sorry her life was cut short because Apollo, in his hubris, thought it took murder and war to save the rest of Olympus. She shouldn't have been a martyr in this cause. She and all the other undead below. I felt sorry for all the women who had been used, mistreated, and had their lives cut short by men. We all deserved better. If I won this damnable game, I'd make sure we *all* got better on Olympus and beyond.

Thetis stopped clawing and snapping at me like a rabid dog and listened. Apparently, I'd said all of that out loud.

"Truce?" I asked.

Thetis nodded. Tears stained her blue cheeks. Her gills and body shuddered with her sobs. "Truce."

Charybdis slowly sank back into the sea. The mind of the sea monster caressed my mental borders. A silent accord made between us.

THIRTY-FOUR

Thankfully, the next corridor we entered had the appearance of the rest of the labyrinth. We treaded the pale stones with the trepidation of those who'd been through an ordeal, cautiously but quickly. Without discussing it, I knew everyone else felt the way I did—The sooner this waking nightmare ended the better.

Confusion struck me. Ahead, I spotted a figure as familiar as the back of my hand. Carlo, in an orange prison jumpsuit, waited with his arms held loosely at his sides. Lines had formed on his forehead that hadn't existed before. Dark circles rimmed his deep brown eyes. His salt and pepper hair had turned white as snow, thinning at the top. His once lean but muscular frame had grown thicker in the middle and thinner, frailer in his limbs. He reminded me of his grandfather.

It didn't make sense. I'd wronged Typhon and Thetis, and they'd wronged me. I'd never wronged Carlo.

Was I blameless? A niggling voice that sounded just like my own asked.

In case something had gotten in my head, I reinforced my mental shields. Also, I checked for cracks in my defenses. There was nothing. It was my own conscious.

"You gave me up, Fran." Carlo shook his head slowly. "I never ratted on you. That was all Apollo. I gave you fair warning they was coming for you, too. You did me wrong in the worse way."

Somehow, I knew his words were true, yet...

Hermes opened his mouth to speak. Athena, Nicky, and Arachne all readied themselves, for what? Then I saw the gleam of metal in his hand.

Carlo had a gun.

"Yes. I gave you up," I agreed, folding my arms across my chest. "I told I.S.E.A. everything to save my skin and clear Luke's name." I held up one finger. "When you left, all we ever were to each other, any ties of family or promises of loyalty were over."

"I was just laying low for a bit." His voice almost had whine to it. The way he'd justify cheating when we were young, or the way he'd justify blowing my divination money on his shady endeavors, before he stopped bothering to justify anything at all.

"The Dear John you left said otherwise."

His nostrils flared. The hand with the gun twitched. "You should have known that was so the cops wouldn't implicate you. I was protecting you."

The letter had served as proof I had no knowledge of the scam. However, I didn't believe this part. Despite not believing him, he had a point. He hadn't ratted on me and in his world that was the most important thing. But to get through this labyrinth, I had to make amends with my enemies.

"I shouldn't have ratted on you. Truce?"

Carlo raised the gun. His hand trembled.

What else could I say to prevent fighting him? I'd apologized. He didn't pull the safety yet. Still, I readied myself to shock him just enough to knock Carlo out.

"Another thing. You made me the bad guy with our son."

I reared my head in genuine shock. This was the first time he'd acknowledged Luke as such.

"You never let me process what he was going through, you know. You poisoned us by not letting me figure out how to accept his transition. We should've gone to a counselor or something. I lost him because of you."

He could've done all that on his own. Apparently, he was having some therapy in prison and regretting his mistakes the way Carlo always regretted them, by blaming others for his behavior. This wasn't his obstacle though. It was mine.

I nodded. "You're right. Counseling would've been better for everyone. Maybe when the games are over, I could arrange for Luke to come see you?"

In his head, I was the one keeping them apart. It would be up to Luke whether he showed up or not. I could try though, so I meant it.

Carlo lowered the gun to his side, using his free hand to wipe his eyes with the back of his hand. "I'd like that. You got yourself a truce."

With that, my ex disappeared.

From that corridor, we came upon a chamber. Waiting in that chamber was Apollo, Artemis, and Hera. Eyeing them as I entered, they seemed as harrowed as I felt.

I didn't want to apologize to him. I'd never done anything wrong to Apollo. Well, not anything I'd apologize for even in this game. I thwarted his plans left and right, and I'd do it again.

However, if he was here, he was done apologizing too, right? Had he examined his mistakes? I decided that wasn't up to me to know. The chamber turned out to be the arena's stage. This was a winner's circle. A tie! It was finally over.

Except, they'd gotten here first...

My heart sank with the realization. Then I noticed something. Everyone from my team was here, but his weren't. Two members were gone.

"They didn't understand the conditions of the game," Apollo said in a quiet voice.

"Cronus was far too angry to ever forgive his son," Hera added, looking at her hands. "Even at the cost of everything."

"Still, I apologize for my role, Lydia. Your mother, your line was dear to me and I—I... I thought if only I could fix this prophecy, change fate, I could revive our world and Mounts Olympus and Orthys to what they once were."

Artemis took a tentative step toward me, then another. "Have you figured out who I am to you?"

I nodded but didn't leave the red circle. I swallowed, realizing who I had to forgive. "Someone my mother used to know."

"Your mother and I should've never been together. We are—we were not the right fit. I thought it would be better to keep my father's eye off your mother by staying away. He used to be quite awful, you see. It is no excuse. I am sorry for abandoning you."

"My grandfather did a good job of being my father," I said, and for the first time, I realized he had. He did his best. He worked hard and gave me a good life. It wasn't his fault he died when I was young. "I forgive you."

"Truce?" Apollo asked.

"Free me of my promise, promise to not start a war on Earth, and it's a deal," I held out my hand.

He held out his hand but didn't shake quite yet. "I promise to not start a war on Earth. Promise to not try to usurp your father, and I free you and yours of any obligation to become a Moirai."

I shook his hand.

WINNER: TEAM RED! flashed above, fireworks went off, but I'd already won.

EPILOGUE

Our wedding wasn't anything like Luke and Juan's affair. Family only. Family included everyone who lived in my household, The Twelve (the original plus Persephone), Thanatos, the harpies, the townsfolk of Milagro Bay, the Supernatural Council of the Americas, and Agents Tan and Roanhorse. Never thought I'd have cops at my wedding, but they assured me that what they did wasn't really police work anymore so much as supernatural social services.

Given Luke was part of their team, I hoped that was true.

Melinoë sent us a wedding gift but declined attending.

Hermes dressed as an Olympian. A golden laurel crown sat upon his head. He was the most handsome god I'd ever laid eyes on. I wore a purple chiton and a golden laurel crown as well.

Athena, not her father, officiated.

We kissed under a trellis loaded with Zeus and Demeter's lavender. The couple decided to remain on Earth. Apollo abdicated his position as king. Hera reclaimed her position of queen—she'd gained a lot of favor with mundanes during the games. I hoped she wouldn't give us trouble down the road.

If she did, I had my own fair share of power and people outside of my pantheon to back me up. However, I think Hera would rather stay away from this world and make peace with her nymph population. We shall see.

I left Clotho, Lachesis, and Atropos, as well as reading anyone's thread, alone. We might have circumstances that change our lives, but it did no one any good to know the future. Because once it's seen, it's believed. Once something is believed, it becomes real—and reality had enough trouble without me poking around in it.

The games were set to happen next year. I'd come back as an officiant to keep my promise, but I certainly wouldn't ever compete again.

Acknowledgments

I'd like to thank Emily Paper (and her thousands of pseudonyms) for her help on this project, forcing me to writing workshops years ago, and for being an auntie to my kids.

I'd also like to thank Karen Dimmick at https://arcanecovers.com/ for her gorgeous cover art on this final book!

About the Author

T.J. Deschamps is a multigenre author writing magical misfits finding family, community, and love one story at a time.

She lives in the Pacific Northwest with her three kids, three cats, and a singular tortoise named Lily. For fun, T.J. likes to hike, lift weights, dance, and read (of course).

If you'd like to hang out with T.J. and her readers, she has a Facebook group called Deschamps Dragons here: https://www.facebook.com/groups/9568669086461680

You can also subscribe to her newsletter and get a free novella Eastside Rock Witch here: https://dl.bookfunnel.com/ovc1vt3mgb

Or, you can follow T.J. on social media.

ALSO BY T.J. DESCHAMPS

Midlife Supernaturals

Eastside Hedge Witch

Eastside Witch Hunt

Eastside Mórrígan

Eastside Coven

Midlife Olympians

Westside Oracle

Westside Harpy

Westside Titan

Westside Titanomachy